'ROO AND THE ANGEL

Furry United Coalition #7

EVE LANGLAIS

E-ISBN: 978 177 38 4035 2
Print ISBN: 978 177 384 0468

PROLOGUE

CLOSE. Getting so close. The science still had a few hiccups —the evidence was in the cages on the second floor.

Still, some failures were expected when embarking on a project of such magnitude.

They were achieving greatness. So what if it broke a few laws? Ignore the fact that some of the subjects—make that all of them—were unwilling. The end game was what mattered.

The money to be made.

The fact that this science, the ability to change mankind, would render them a god.

And someone had dared to attack a god in the making. Dared to question the work.

They would pay. But not with their lives. There were better uses for those opposing him. Better tasks suited to the Jones boys such as empty cages that could use fresh specimens.

Muahahahahaha.

"ARE YOU AN ANGEL?" The question emerged from the man standing in front of Nevaeh's cage. He didn't just stand there, though. He stared at her. At least she assumed he stared. Hard to tell what his eyes were doing behind his shaded goggles. The fact he wore them inside gave her an insane urge to sing a certain song by Corey Hart.

The stranger, dressed in mercenary black from head to toe, wasn't someone she'd ever seen here before and, given he didn't wear the usual company uniform, offered a slight beacon of hope.

"Let me out." The words emerged more like an order than a plea. He didn't immediately react, and Nevaeh had to wonder if he heard her. Or if he even cared.

Why should he? After all, it wasn't as if the doctors and scientists and guards in this place ever paid her wishes, or her rights, any mind.

Bastards. *I hope you all catch something awful.* A virulent disease that would have them pooping out their innards and dying a disgusting death. She'd seen it before. It wasn't pretty.

"Hello? Earth to stranger." She snapped her fingers impatiently when he didn't reply.

He pushed the goggles up onto his forehead, shoving his hair up into spikes. He did indeed stare at her with bright, brown eyes set in a rock-hewn face, the kind that showed no expression, no emotion. No compassion.

The one thing she was fairly certain of was he didn't belong in this place. For one, he actually looked at her and not through her, but more importantly, he didn't have the same smell as the others. No decontamination baths for him. Rather, he stank of smoke and gunpowder. Was he part of the group attacking this place? She'd woken to the welcome sound of weapons' fire and explosions while the screams had her fervently wishing all the douchetards in this place came to a permanent end.

And I hope it hurt.

They deserved it for hurting her.

As for the stranger, she'd yet to ascertain, rescuer or executioner? Since coming to this place, she could no longer tell people's intentions. Even the kindest smile sometimes hid a devious agenda. The doctors pretended to be friendly even as they plotted—and experimented.

And when those test subjects didn't quite turn out as expected? The institute knew how to keep a secret and wasn't afraid to eliminate mistakes. They had to, given what they did inside these locked walls was illegal and immoral. Those scientists, who pretended to not hear the pleas for mercy, had to hide their actions. Hide their sick agenda.

Mixing people with animals. What the hell was that about? Why would anyone want to create hybrid monsters?

One doctor claimed it was the future of mankind. Um,

hello. Had that idiot never read a book or watched a movie?

The world would never accept people who weren't normal. Would never live alongside those who were different.

Those were the ones the institute considered failures. The successful ones? Those were the ones who made it through the experiments with their changes hidden. Invisible, yet present if needed. Some of the test subjects could control the shifts in their DNA, looking human one second, full animal the next. She'd seen it with her own eyes. Those were considered a success.

Others, like those kept on this level, in this section, inside the long row of cages, couldn't hide their extra parts. Like Rory and his furry mane, which might not have been so bad if it weren't for his whiskers, the tufted tail, and the fact he couldn't talk, only roar. Which got tiresome after a while.

Then there was Lump—one big blob of a man—and Snake with his yellow-slitted stare and forked tongue. They didn't look human and even now warbled and hissed at the man standing sentinel with a gun slung over his shoulder.

A man who wouldn't stop staring at her.

Staring at her wings.

"Take a picture. It will last longer," she snapped, annoyed by his rudeness. Then again, what did she expect?

Unlike Lump and the rest, Nevaeh looked human. She had all her toes and fingers, the face in mirrors still her own. But she could never walk down a city street again, not with what they'd done to her.

She'd never be free.

5

His hands went to his ears, and he popped out a plug before saying in a low voice. "Hi."

Hi? He ogled a woman in a cage and that was all he could say?

Someone was a little fascinated and tongue-tied, which was why she approached the bars and gave him her best damsel-in-distress expression. "Help me. Please." She even added a trembling lower lip—rather than an upraised middle finger.

He visibly started and asked again, "Are you an angel?"

Not quite. Although she could understand his confusion, what with those things sticking out of her back. Wings, great big ones. Thankfully, she didn't have a halo to go with them. Not even close, although, in a twist of irony, her actual name was Nevaeh, which was heaven spelled backwards. But her parents couldn't have known when she was born what would eventually happen to her.

"Do I look like a do-gooder angel?" she asked.

"You have wings."

"Really? I hadn't noticed," she replied with a sarcastic lilt.

"I guess that was rude of me to point out."

"You think?" She arched a brow. "How would you like it if I pointed out the fact you have a scar by your lip?"

"You'd just be proving what my dad says, that chicks dig scars."

Her lips pressed flat. "I am not a chick, nor am I digging anything. You, obviously, get off on seeing a woman in a cage."

"Actually, you're my first."

"Bet you haven't said that in a while," she grumbled.

"You would be right." The corner of his lip lifted, and

she was stunned by the realization he flirted with her. The distant sound of gunfire snapped her back to her reality.

"Can you get me out of here?"

He approached the bars and, before she could give him warning, placed his hands on them.

Sizzle. As the current coursed through his flesh, he did a little jiggle, his eyes widened, and his hair lifted. He flung himself back and shook his hands. "Holy lizard on a hot plate. They electrified the bars."

A lesson all the prisoners quickly learned. "I was about to warn you."

"Warning me would have been shouting, 'Don't touch.'"

"Don't touch."

He glared.

She shrugged. "Don't be a baby about it. You're still alive."

"My hands are burning."

"I know. It will go away after awhile." She knew from experience. "Can you deactivate it and let me out?"

"Who are you?" he asked instead.

She might have said something rude—along the lines of your worse fucking nightmare if you don't release me— except Rory the freakin' lion chose that moment to let out a pitiful roar. More like a cat that got its tail stepped on, but enough to draw the guy's attention. He turned away, giving her a view of an ass that looked remarkably fine in those cargo pants. However now was not the time to admire his butt. He was the first person since her capture to actually see her. Talk to her without using the words, "Hold still while we take some blood." He represented the only chance she'd seen thus far to escape.

"Ignore him. He's always meowing."

The stranger's gaze swung back to her. "Is he stuck like that?"

"You think we want to look like freaks?"

"You're not freaks."

The emphasis narrowed her gaze and roused some doubt. "Are you with *them*?" Them as in the dicks who ran this place.

"If you're implying I had a part in this, then no. Not even close."

"Then why are you here?"

"I'm looking for my brother and his girlfriend."

"Do they work here?"

He shook his head. "They were taken prisoner recently."

"New test subjects."

"Have you seen them?"

"In case you hadn't noticed, my view is rather limited. If they're not in this room, then no."

"Bugger. Give me a sec would you." He shoved his earpiece back in and tapped it. "Second level, west section, no sign of Jax and his chick."

Definitely not one of the guards then. "Let me out and I'll help you look." She'd keep an eye out as she fled for the nearest exit.

"You'll be free soon enough, Angel. Rescue is coming."

"Don't you mean more cages and more doctors?" Her lip curled. "I'm not stupid. You and I both know me and my buddies in this here room won't be set free. Heck, the chances of me living another week are pretty slim." Because the world could never know what happened here.

He didn't even deny it. "Those that can be rehabilitated will be set free."

"You mean those that look human."

He stepped closer. "Can you hide your wings?"

She fluttered them. "Exactly how would you suggest I do that? If I could hide them, I wouldn't be on this level with the freaks." At the hiss from her more feline jail companion, she tossed a casual, "Sorry, Rory, but it's true. They only keep what they call the failures here."

The remark made the newcomer's lips flatten. "I take it you weren't always like this."

What a stupid remark. "What do you think?" Despite the fact he was her only hope of escape, she couldn't help the sarcasm.

"Do the wings work? I mean, can you actually fly?"

She shrugged. "No idea. It's not as if the doctors ever let me out to try." Probably afraid she'd never come back. Probably right on that score. It didn't help that the last time she'd gotten out of her cage there'd been an incident. The kind that involved a body bag.

A siren sounded, kind of late in the grand scheme of things. She might not have paid it much mind except she noted the far end of the hall where the stranger had entered was filling with a green gas.

"Um, buddy, I think we might have a problem."

Turning, he cursed. "Shit. Someone must have managed to hit a panic button. Jay was supposed to disable those."

"Any idea what it is?" she asked, eyeing the green haze as it hit the first row of cells.

"Probably not good."

"Duh, Sherlock," she muttered as he walked partway up the hall lined with cages, stopping well out of reach of the gas.

Whatever he saw had him jogging back. He stood in

front of the panel for the locks on the cages. A panel flashing red.

"What's happening?" she asked, creeping as close as she dared to the bars.

"Looks like they're getting rid of the evidence."

A polite way of saying someone wanted to kill the liabilities. She glanced toward the other end of the room, and her jaw dropped as she noted bodies slumping in their cages. Not a single cry emerged from them. Not a single squeak as they hit the floor, and then...

"They're turning into puddles!" she yelled.

"Aw, hell. This is not good. Hold on, Angel. I'm gonna try and bust you out of here." He rammed the butt of his gun into the panel, smashing the red lights, which caused lots of pretty sparks but did nothing to open the cages.

The mist crept closer.

"Do something!" she screeched.

"What would you like me to do?" he hollered back. "I don't have a code or a key."

"Use your gun."

He looked down at his weapon and shook his head. "Bad idea. The bullets could ricochet. I think I might have something better." He reached into a pocket and pulled out a small chunk of something dark. He shoved it against the cage, and she caught on to his plan. "Stand back."

No need to tell her twice. She dove into the corner, ducked her face in to it, her wings covering her like a shield.

Boom.

The explosion vibrated her entire body, including her teeth. When she turned around, the door to her cage hung drunkenly, and he beckoned. "Hurry. We haven't much time.

The green mist had reached the cell before hers. Empty of subjects, but no less ominous. She sprinted for the opening, the mangled metal not moving, her wings getting caught in the cramped crevice.

"I'm stuck," she gasped.

LH—her nickname for the guy she thought of as Last Hope—shoved at the twisted door, grunting with the effort while she stared at the creeping deadly fog.

With a scream of tortured metal, it moved, and she slid through, just in time. The mist licked at her cell as they headed for the door. A door that wouldn't open at his shove. He cursed.

"It's locked," she observed.

"I see that. And I don't have any explosives left." He tapped at his ear. "Hey. If you're listening, I need your help now. Get the door for my section unlocked."

He frowned and replied to a voice she couldn't hear. "No this can't wait, unless you want to explain to Da why you let his favorite son turn into a meat puddle."

LH pressed himself against the wall and drew Nevaeh beside him, both of them staring at the creeping fog. He kept up his one-sided conversation. "You can have whatever you like from my collection. Just get this door fucking open."

"No. I won't say it." His lips pressed tight. She pressed against him, looking to escape the mist curling close to their toes.

The guy sighed and said, "Fine. You win. You are the handsomest of the Joneses and the best brother ever in the whole wide fucking world. Now open the godsdamned door!"

Click. The door gave suddenly, the electronic lock

releasing. They wasted no time spilling into the next hall, slamming the door shut behind them.

"I am going to put itching powder in his boots," LH grumbled.

"I hope you don't mean the guy who saved our lives."

"Don't be fooled. My brother is a dick," he grumbled as he took stock of their new location.

Brother? Was this some kind of family operation? Did it matter? He'd gotten her out of the cage.

They found themselves in a huge lab. An empty lab. The scientists who usually worked here either gone or hiding.

Come out, come out, wherever you are. She wouldn't mind having a word with them, without the bars in the way.

Her rescuer didn't seem interested in searching for the staff. He dragged her past the counters with their beakers and vials. Past the bed with the straps where she'd spent quite a bit of time; before the wings. After the wings, she couldn't exactly lie down easily.

Her rescuer tapped his ear and began talking again. "Tell the boys to stay away from Section 3B. No idea how long it will take for the gas to clear."

Who was he? And whom did he report to?

She didn't dare ask but listened, trying to gather as much information as she could.

"The subjects?" His voice held a questioning note as he eyed her. Someone must have asked him if he'd found any. Nevaeh did her best to look afraid—which she wasn't—harmless—which she also wasn't—and shook her head. A silent plea.

"The gas killed them all. And you can forget bodies. Whatever they used turned them into puddles of goo."

A reminder that she'd almost died, too.

She mouthed a thank you, but he didn't lose his grim look. He tapped his ear, shutting off his mic and said, "Don't thank me yet, Angel. We still need to get you out of here because you are right. If anyone sees you, they will take you into custody."

"One prison for another." Her shoulders slumped.

"Not if I have anything to say about it." He moved to a window set in the wall and peeked out. He gestured to her.

"I've got to go help my brothers clear this place. In the next few minutes there will a lot of chaos. Perhaps even enough to hide the fact you're escaping to those woods over there." He pointed to a scraggly copse of trees.

"You're leaving me?"

"I don't have a choice. You can't come with me."

She almost asked why not. He was the first person she'd met since her change to treat her normally. To not look at her wings and wonder how to use them. "What am I supposed to do in the woods?"

"Wait until dark to move."

"Move where?" She didn't mean to say it out loud.

"Somewhere safer than here."

The look she tossed him? Totally deserved, as was her stinging retort. "Safer? Where am I supposed to go? I'm a freak."

"You're beautiful."

Of the pair of them, she couldn't have said who appeared more surprised. She ignored the compliment and chose to remark on her reality. "I have nowhere to go. No way to hide what they did to me. Maybe I should just turn myself in."

"No!" he barked. He softened his next words. "Do you trust me?"

She didn't trust anyone.

He read her expression and for some reason appeared angry. "I'm one of the good guys, Angel. Kind of. I promise I won't hurt you. Give me a chance to help you."

"Help me how?"

"I don't know yet. For the moment, stay in the woods and wait for me."

"What if you don't come back?"

"I'll come. But you gotta go now. Before someone sees you."

Leave?

He thrust his gun at her. "Take this to protect yourself."

A gun? "I don't know how to use it."

"Point it in the general direction and pull the trigger. But only if you can't run."

"Thank you. But I can protect myself." She shoved the gun back at him. Then, on impulse, she pressed a kiss to his lips. An electrical embrace that had them both gasping.

She drew away, and he quirked his lips. "Now that's what I call incentive. Stay safe, Angel. I'll be back soon."

Then he took off for the far end of the room and the door. A door that led to the main part of the building and the chaos she could still hear.

How was she supposed to escape? The way behind them was full of poison. The door he'd used would result in her getting caught, leaving only...

She eyed the window and sighed.

I hate heights. Always had. Took drugs to knock her out before every flight. She couldn't go to sleep now, and she didn't have much of a choice.

A nearby chair provided a handy tool to smash the window. Crash. She couldn't help but wince at the noise. A subtle peek outside showed no one below.

She spent a moment picking out the shards in the frame, gearing herself up for the next step, which involved perching on the windowsill, trying to not lose the contents of her tummy as the ground appeared dizzyingly far below.

It's only one floor.

People broke bones at smaller heights.

I have wings.

That she'd never used to fly.

The gunfire got closer. As did the shouts of men.

Are you going to let them capture you again?

Hell no.

I have wings. How hard can it be to fly?

She jumped out.

Turned out flying was harder than it looked. *Crunch.*

2

LEAVING THE ANGEL—*HOLY shit, I found an angel!*—wasn't sitting well with Jeb. What choice did he have? He couldn't take her with him because she was right about one thing. If anyone saw her, they'd lock her away under the guise of keeping the secret of shapeshifters safe.

The people he used to work for—the shifter version of special ops military, aka FUC—weren't known for being compassionate when it came to keeping the truth of cryptids from humans. Which meant if they couldn't hide what she was, they'd eliminate her.

I can't allow that to happen.

Since he no longer technically worked for them, and was here as a brother and independent contractor, Jeb felt very few qualms about telling her to escape. How could he do anything else once he saw those vivid violet eyes?

Everything about her struck him like a fist to the gut. From her shoulder-length, red, bobbed hair framing a pixie-ish face—and yes, a man could use the word pixie-ish—to her short toned legs peeking from under her gown. When you'd lived in the outback all your life, you got to know about more creatures than they taught in school or on television specials. The angel possessed a tiny frame, one that seemed too light to carry those massive wings, and yet her every movement was graceful. She was utterly beautiful.

And obviously not human.

Despite him urging her to escape, the reality was she wouldn't make it far. The place would soon be crawling with FUC operatives—short for Furry United Coalition—who would leave no experiment—even the angelic-looking ones—to wander. She would be caught and put in a cage for processing. There was no way of avoiding it. Jeb just didn't have the heart to tell her. What he could do was ensure someone else took her into custody. *At least it won't be me.*

Maybe he'd be allowed to visit her. Surely, she'd like that. She had, after all, kissed him. He wouldn't mind kissing her again.

Something to worry about later. There was still a mission to complete.

He ran into his brother Jeremy in the next hallway.

His older sibling, a darker-haired version of him with a scowl, asked, "Where the heck you been? We located Jax and his birdie."

"They're safe?" Jeb asked.

"Yup, but we haven't laid eyes on Kole yet. He might have already flown the coop." The wily koala kept evading them while continuing his devious plans that involved experimenting on living people. The Jones brothers were determined to see Kole fail.

His earpiece came to life as Jaycon—another of his brothers—barked from the other end. "Get your arses outside. A helicopter just landed in a nearby field. We think Kole is about to make a run for it."

Jeb tapped his earpiece and replied. "We'll make our way outside, but doubtful we'll get there in time."

"Good thing I've got a bird on its way to your location. ETA, two minutes. So haul arse."

"We're moving." He and Jeremy jogged down the hall toward the opposite end and another set of stairs. Jeb ignored the bodies on the way. The time spent in the shifter special forces meant he understood sometimes lethal outcomes couldn't be avoided. On the contrary, when it came to keeping their secret, he—a veritable kangaroo that human scientists would drool over— couldn't show compassion.

Which was why he could so easily lie to Angel. Truth was, he didn't want anything to happen to her. He really didn't. But he had a duty to not only the Shifter Council that regulated the actions of all shifters but his family. He wouldn't do anything to jeopardize them.

Most of the time.

Hitting the main floor, they ran into Jakob and Uncle Kendrick. The first with even more scars for chicks to dig, and the second a grizzled version of themselves later in life.

"Jaycon says to get our hairy butts outside," Jeb stated as he kept moving past them, looking for a door out of the building.

"We heard. Something about a helicopter and a field."

"Which is this way, numbskull." Uncle Kendrick jabbed his finger in the opposite direction Jeb had decided on.

"I knew that," he mumbled.

It didn't take long before they made their way back

through the doors they'd blasted open. The institute with its illegal experiments had stiff security, but nothing the Jones boys couldn't handle.

Heading outside, Jeb heard the distant sound of the whirring blades. As he turned the corner of the building, the wind whipped at his hair. More astonishing was the sight of a bird, no a lizard, no a...

"What the heck is that?" he asked as the giant creature on two legs with a long neck and a ridged crest atop its head chased after a small man.

Jeremy snickered. "It's Jax's girlfriend."

"I thought she was an ostrich." Jeb couldn't help his confusion.

"Only until she gets mad. Then she's prehistoric and deadly. Lucky bastard."

"Is that Kole she's chasing?" Jeb asked, tracking the movements of the man, wondering if he changed into his 'roo, could he catch him in time? Not likely given he made a sudden move toward a waiting helicopter. Shots fired veered the prehistoric bird away from the metal machine. It lifted from the ground, and as it did, a face peeked out of it.

"Ah shit. There she is," muttered Jakob. "See that woman on the chopper?" He pointed.

Jeb squinted at the woman in red, clinging to the door-frame of the helicopter. A woman who seemed vaguely familiar. "Who is that?"

"Mum."

The words almost caused him to face-plant. Only his brother yanking him by the arm kept him upright.

"Mum? But she's dead," he blustered as his brother kept tugging him toward a dangling ladder. A second heli-copter hovered overhead.

"Apparently not. That bloke Kole's got her, and we've got to rescue her."

The swaying ladder just about slapped him in the face as he tossed another look over his shoulder. Surely his brother was wrong. Their mother had died in an unfortunate outback incident. One that almost took their brother Jaxon, too. They'd found him over twenty years ago in a dingo den with only scraps left of their mother's summer dress.

Her body was never found.

Until now. Alive and well. What the bloody hell was going on?

Jeb grabbed hold of the ladder and clambered upward to the cabin where a few of his brothers were already waiting; Jeremy and Jakob. His Uncle Kyle piloted it, eyes shaded behind aviator glasses.

The helicopter lurched to the side as soon as they'd boarded but, before taking off after their target, made one more stop, dangling the ladder over Jax on the ground.

"Move your fat ass," joked Jaycon as Jax began to climb, the brothers speeding the process by reeling in the ladder. Then they were off.

The helicopter dipped, heading full speed after the black one holding Kole—and Mum. The blades were painted crimson and provided a blur of color against the blue sky. Jeb only half listened as his brothers discussed the odd turn of events.

"...place is a fuckin' horror house," exclaimed Jax. "You should have seen what they were keeping in a walk-in freezer. Jars and bags of body parts."

"Ha. That's nothing. You should have seen the shit they were growing in these big cylinders filled with fluid. The one with eyeballs was watching me, I swear."

Each of his brothers had a tale to tell, but Jeb kept his mouth shut. The demise of the hybrids by the gas was a sad thing. They'd obviously not asked for their fate. As for Angel… He now wondered if he'd done the right thing. Perhaps he should have stuck with her. Helped her get to safety.

A slap upside his head snapped him out of his reverie. "Hey, dumbass, what freaky shit did you see?"

Since he couldn't tell them he'd found an angel, he stuck to something they'd like. "The blob." Which set his brothers off on another tangent of horror movies.

Meanwhile, he wanted to know more about the woman who looked like Mum. He leaned close to Jeremy and said, "Why would Mum be with Kole?" Was she a prisoner? Must be. She'd never leave her baby boys.

His older brother shrugged. "No idea. And we're not even sure it's her. Could just be someone that looks like her. Our primary target remains Kole. We can't let the furry twerp escape."

Except Kole had come to this fight better prepared than them. Their helicopter swerved suddenly to the left, sending the Jones boys sliding and scrambling to hold on lest they fall out the open door. Seatbelts were for pussies.

Another tilt jerked them to the other side.

"Uncle K, what the fuck?" Jeremy yelled.

"They're shooting bloody missiles at us!" exclaimed their uncle.

"Who?" Jeremy leaned forward to peer, whereas Jeb peeked out the side and noted that, while Kole's helicopter still scooted away from them, coming in rapidly on both sides, two more birds in the sky!

Matte black, military grade, and armed.

"Shit!" It was pretty much a universal exclamation as

their uncle dipped and swerved, dropped and rose, avoiding the converging fire from the other two choppers.

The boys weren't idle, though. Jaycon and Jeremy set up in either door, guns braced, their bodies held steady by their siblings.

Rat-tat-tat. Tat-rat-rat. There was a whoop when one of the enemy choppers began to list, smoke pouring from its tail. Jeb, his hand stuck through the loop of his brother Jeremy's belt, watched as it sank lower and lower, smashing into the ground. Then it exploded.

One down.

The boys cheered, and yet the danger was far from over. The other chopper harried them, though Uncle did his best to avoid it. His brothers did their part as well, firing on it. Hitting it. The other helicopter wobbled in the air then came straight at them. Which would have been fine, except they were being pinched by a mountain on one side. Uncle yanked the stick and tried to rise, but the other helicopter, more powerful, rose faster and broke even. Jeremy took aim at the cockpit of the other vessel and scored a direct hit, which would have been cause to rejoice, except, without a pilot, the other chopper listed right into them, the blades tangling with a screech of metal.

Their uncle cursed as they began to drop.

The Jones brothers didn't scream and go crashing to their fate. Once again, their special ops training took over. They dove out of the door closest to the mountain and prayed. Jeb's fingers scrabbled for purchase, scraping and sliding on rock, the toes of his boots searching for even the hint of a ledge. A chunk of rock slid away before he found a spot.

But it was better than being in the chopper when it

landed with a *boom* and exploded. Smoke rose in the air, a beacon for searchers.

That was how the FUC found them, clinging to the mountainside, holding onto every branch and rock that would support them.

A face peered over the cliff edge, bright eyed and entirely too cheerful. She exclaimed, "You boys need a hand?"

Thankfully the FUC agents who'd been trailing them on the ground, having arrived late to the fight—on purpose because a certain Jones might have given them the wrong time—had some rope in their Range Rover. What they didn't have was enough room for all the brothers.

Which was why Jeb volunteered to hop back to the compound. Partially in the hope he could avoid any accusation in Angel's eyes when the FUC agents found her.

Only when he finally did make it onto the property did he discover the only people recovered alive had been Jax and Mari. All the other test subjects were dead or gone.

Including his angel.

3

THE PEOPLE SEARCHING the grounds came close to her tree. Almost as if they followed a trail, but a shout had them veering before they could find her, and Nevaeh heaved a sigh of relief.

Free still, for the moment. And alive. Barely.

While her first attempt at flying had been a colossal failure, she at least didn't break anything. Bruise herself? Yes. Especially her pride, but she was alive and able to limp to the woods, expecting at any moment for someone to find her.

Shoot her in the back.

Taser her, which wasn't as funny as in the movies. The whole jiggling-body thing really freaking hurt.

However, she made it to the cover of the trees relatively unscathed and then climbed one, hiding herself among the boughs to watch. From her hidden perch, peeking through branches, she saw the helicopters swooping on the other side of the building then racing off. Wondered if her rescuer was aboard.

Wondered if he'd ever come back.

Not that she cared. *I don't need him or anyone else.*

With that stubborn thought in mind, she stayed in that tree for hours, listening as more people arrived, spilling out of cars and trucks, not making any attempt to hide their presence. Curiosity drew her to a tree closer to the edge of the clearing, a tall one that gave her an excellent view.

Perched amidst the boughs and leaves, she spied, noting the new arrivals were dressed in street clothes, not a black uniform among them. They entered the building, exiting minutes later with arms full of boxes or laden with computers. Emptying the place of its knowledge, to what purpose?

Are they the good or bad guys? She couldn't exactly tell, especially since her rescuer didn't appear among them.

Not knowing who they were or what they intended, she kept out of sight.

Darkness fell, and still she huddled in her tree, belly tight with hunger, with nothing to chew on but her own stupid thoughts. Unable to help herself from remembering how it all started.

I just wanted to make some extra money.

What person in their twenties, who dropped out of school and preferred a vagabond lifestyle, didn't want to make a few extra bucks? The offer was printed in black and white in a newspaper. The ad didn't give any warning of how replying would change her life.

Are you tired of being ordinary? Do you long to spread real wings and fly? Become something more? Something special...

Dorky claims. However, it was the small text underneath that intrigued her.

Chosen applicants will receive accommodations, meals, and generous remuneration for their time.

Ka-ching. Whatever it was, it paid, and she could use the dough.

As for what were they looking for?

The Bunyip Institute wanted healthy young men and women, ages eighteen to twenty-five, for some kind of scientific study. Having done this kind of thing before—sleep studies, food tasting, egg donation—she kind of knew what to expect. Several rounds of testing. Each one paid.

The Bunyip Institute proved no different at first. Round one was where she filled in the questionnaire.

Name: Nevaeh Karson

Occupation: Bartender (Which seemed better than mentioning she was a vagabond with no fixed address.)

Family: ~~Assholes.~~ Unavailable.

And so on… For her current address, she used the gym that she'd stolen a pass for so she could shower.

The money from the ten-page quiz—which asked detailed health questions, including the date of her last period—paid for a room above a laundromat for one month. A steady roof over her head was a fist-pump moment.

Round two was the physical portion. It involved her doing all kinds of sweaty stuff like running on a treadmill —*"I'm not a bloody hamster."*—while someone measured her blood pressure. She had to do a stamina test, which she did well on mostly because she walked almost everywhere she went. Street-smart girls knew better than to hitch rides. She swam, held her breath underwater, did a paltry number of chin-ups, and squatted until her thighs burned. Not exactly her idea of fun, yet it paid enough that she could afford to eat. Good stuff, too. Not things scrounged from other people's plates. Amazing what people walked away from in the food courts at the mall.

She passed with flying colors and made it to round three. The MRI and extensive lab work testing her blood and organs had her doctor absolutely giddy.

"You are a perfect candidate," Dr. Guffo exclaimed from behind his owl-like lenses. The giant, blinking orbs freaked her out, as did his odd enthusiasm over her rare AB negative blood type. But his science-boner was easy to ignore when he handed her another check with several zeros. She agreed to the next and final round of their study.

All the testing led to her sitting in a pure white room within the downtown location for the Bunyip Institute, a futuristic glass and chrome building with a lobby full of television screens all showing perfect, model-type people talking about tomorrow and how wonderful it would be.

Blah, blah, marketing crap. She paid no mind to it. The institute promised to make people's lives better. So long as they paid her, she was cool with whatever they did.

Stepping inside, she'd felt out of place with her duffel bag stuffed with clothes and personal items for what they called an "extended stay." Because, congrats, she'd made it to the final round. The security guard in the reception area eyed her sternly, but the woman behind the desk smiled warmly.

"You must be one of our lucky candidates. Welcome."

Finally, a winner.

About time.

I wish I'd known it was a booby prize.

Nev could still remember snapping a piece of bubblegum as she waited her turn on the sixth floor.

Bored. Impatient. What was the point of making her show up at a specific time only to make her cool her heels?

It didn't help that the room she'd been told to park her butt in had three other applicants, each of them called into the next room one at a time, until only she remained.

When this is over, I'm going to use the money I make to pay my rent for six months and go back to school. Maybe finally get a degree in something so she could get a real job instead of part-time stuff here and there. Plant some real roots. What a concept.

A muffled scream lifted her head. Odd.

When it didn't repeat, she dipped her gaze down and kept browsing *YouTube* on her phone. Another item she'd splurged on with her newfound earnings, and lucky her, the institute had free Wi-Fi.

A distant shout was followed by... She frowned. Was that a roar? As in an animal roaring? Unexpected given she thought they only did testing on people.

But she wasn't going to quibble about it. They paid too well for that. Besides, if she was willing to let them test on her, then she couldn't very well complain about animals. The place was obviously legit. The big, shiny, chrome and glass building nestled in the heart of the city catered to the rich and famous, or so the media propaganda on the screens claimed.

The door opened, and Dr. Guffo emerged, his glasses askew on his nose, his hair tousled, his expression slightly frazzled. "Ah, there you are."

"Where else would I be?" Sarcasm, her best friend.

"Nowhere of course. Ha. Ha." He gave a nervous chuckle. "Shall we?"

Snaring her duffel bag, Nev followed him into a small room with a curtained cubicle and a pile of bags. Those of the peeps who'd gone before her. She dumped hers on top but kept her phone.

The doctor shook his head. "You can't use that here. Sensitive equipment."

She frowned as he held out his hand.

"I promise, no one will steal it."

They wouldn't be stealing much. She'd bought it off a guy on the street for fifty bucks. She handed it over, and the doctor placed it atop her bag.

"If you would please change." He indicated the cubicle, and she didn't bother grumbling. Medical places always insisted on patients, even voluntary ones, wearing those stupid tissue gowns. It didn't take long to shed her gear and put it on, the scratchy paper making her nipples poke.

She held her clothes against her chest to hide them, but Dr. Guffo wasn't looking as she exited. He had his tablet in hand and was busy sliding his finger over it.

She dumped her stuff on top of her phone then gripped the gown in a way that wouldn't flash her ass to everyone.

"Ready?" he said, looking up from his screen. "Excellent. If you'll just follow me through here."

He placed his hand on a square, dark screen. It lit blue, and she heard a click before the door slid open giving them access.

Entering, Nevaeh immediately saw the bed, the medical type with raised metal railings. It was the straps that gave her pause.

"You going to tie me down or something?"

The doctor gave her a little shove to move her forward. She stumbled as he entered the room and the door slid shut behind him. "Just a precaution so you don't flinch when we give you the treatment."

"This won't hurt, right? No one said anything about this hurting."

"Not one bit."

So why wouldn't he look her in the eye when saying it?

"How long is this part of the testing supposed to take? And when do I get paid?"

"When we're done, which should be about two weeks. Then, if the testing goes well, you'll have the option of extending the treatment."

"For more money, right?" Although she began to wonder if perhaps this would be the last thing she'd volunteer for. Things were getting a little freaky even for her.

"You will be rewarded for your time and effort. Now if you would please lie down."

In retrospect, she was much like that stupid lamb that skipped willingly to the slaughter. She put herself in that bed. Didn't struggle at all when the straps went around her wrists and then her ankles. She did begin to breathe faster when the thick one wound around her torso.

When the doctor approached with the giant needle, trepidation hit her hard.

But it was too late.

Hell, the moment she volunteered to be a test subject it was too late. They saw something in her they wanted. And what the institute coveted, they took.

When next she woke, her new world consisted of pain.

And more pain.

But it was weeks, perhaps even months, before she was lucid enough to realize what they'd done to her.

To discover the monster they'd made her into. To realize they'd removed her chance at a normal life. That they—

"Angel?" The hushed whisper startled her from her sleep where she relived the nightmare of how she'd gotten her wings. It wasn't as sweet or gentle as the ringing of a bell.

She crouched on her branch and stared down at the ground, the darkness pressing in on all sides.

"Angel? Are you here? Answer me if you are."

He'd come for her? Nev had not actually believed the stranger would. She'd hidden in the woods mostly because she had no better plan.

But he'd returned. Why?

She watched as he crept through the forest, pretty quiet for a man his size. Obviously a fellow who knew how to sneak.

Who was he? In the rush of being rescued she'd never thought to wonder what his motive was in invading the laboratory. *He did say he was looking for his brother.* But at the same time, he was well prepared. Armed. Dressed to kill. He even had explosives. Obviously not your regular Joe Blow.

Was he part of some government agency looking to put an end to the crime happening in the lab? Or was he working for another asshole who'd just want to use her to do further experiments on humans?

She didn't make a sound. Not a single peep, and yet suddenly he was looking right up at her.

"Hey, Angel."

How could he see her? It was pitch-black. She could see him plain as day, part of her special modifications. Changed her eye color when they did it. Bye bye, brown eyes. Hello, purple.

Yes, purple. As if having wings didn't make her strange enough.

"How did you know I was here?"

"Because you're easy to see," he remarked. "Did you know your eyes glow in the dark?"

"They do not!" she exclaimed.

"They totally do. Reminds me of Halloween."

For some reason, this ruffled her feathers. "Are you calling me scary?"

"What? No." Good thing she could see his genuinely appalled expression. "It's rather pretty. And I love it. Um, Halloween that is. Because of the lollies." The dark couldn't hide the heat in his cheeks.

She cocked her head. "Why did you come back?"

"I told you I would."

Her lips pursed. "But you didn't actually expect to find me, did you?"

For a second, she thought he'd lie. Instead he sighed. "No, I didn't. Figured you'd get caught actually."

"If you thought that, then why are you in the woods?"

"Because they're combing the place right now looking for evidence and survivors. Of the first, they've found some, but the latter…" He shook his head.

"Most of them were moved. The successful ones that is. Day before last."

"And they didn't take you with them?" he asked.

She shook her head, realized he might not see it and replied. "I'm not considered a success story."

"How can you not be? You have wings."

Which was something that had initially excited the scientists, until they realized she couldn't do anything to hide them. Apparently, they wanted her to be like the successful stories that could flip in and out of beast mode at will.

"I was considered a failure."

"Then they were dumb." Vehemently spoken.

"They were right. I can't go anywhere with these." The wings at her back rustled. "I should have stayed in the lab to get melted with the others."

"You don't mean that."

For a moment, she almost let him think she was indulging in a pity party, and then she snickered. "No. I'll figure out a way to survive. Maybe find a doctor who can remove them."

"Remove them?" He sounded aghast. His mouth dropped open. "How can you say that? They're a part of you."

"Well, I'd rather they weren't." She leapt down from the tree, expecting to hit the ground, only hands—big, firm hands—caught her midair.

He lowered her slowly to the ground, and she was torn about how she felt about it. How long since anyone touched her without causing pain? Had offered her help?

How long since the touch of a man made her flesh tingle?

The stranger took his time releasing her, and she proved just as slow stepping back.

"Do you have somewhere to go?" he asked. "Someone you can call?"

Her nose wrinkled. "If you're talking about family, then no. The only one left alive is my dad, and he's a drunk." One with a quick temper and heavy fist.

"Surely you have friends you can call. I'll bet ass could help you."

Her jaw dropped. "Excuse me? What's that supposed to mean? I'm not some kind of whore who sells her body to people."

His turn to look aghast. "What are you talking about,

33

Angel? I never implied that. I meant ass as in the Avian Soaring Security department. If you can't reconnect with your flock or whatever nest you belong to, then ass could probably help."

"Ha. Ha. Very funny." She crossed her arms over her chest. "I'm glad you think my having wings is a joke. Guess I should get used to being the butt of them from you normal people."

"Us normal people?" he queried. His expression appeared confused and then thoughtful. "Angel, before the institute, could you fly?"

"In a plane."

"So you never had wings?"

She snorted. "Of course not."

"Beak? Feathers?"

Her annoyance grew with each stupid question. "You're a jerk." She whirled and began to stomp away, not sure of where she was going, barefoot, with only the hospital gown draped over her front, with cotton shorts for a bottom. But damned if she was going to stand around having him accuse her of being some kind of bird. She wasn't a bird. She was—

"You're human," he stated.

"No duh, Sherlock," she spat, not turning to look back. "What else would I be? Have been," she amended. "And we all know how humanity treats those who are different. You being a prime example. Making jokes about my deformity." And reinforcing her belief she'd never have a normal life again. "Maybe I should just turn myself in. Become a lab bird for the rest of my life." Perch on a stick in a cage and chirp for crackers.

"You are not giving up."

"What else is there to do? Live in the woods? Make myself a nest and dig for grubs to eat?"

"Why eat bugs when you can forage for edible stuff?"

"And just what is edible?" She gestured to the towering trees and the bushes. "Maybe you know how to live off the land, but I don't. I'd probably poison myself within a day. Die of dehydration." End up with diarrhea and wiping her ass with something that would leave a rash.

Sob.

Overwhelmed, tears threatened, and a tremor struck her limbs, striking at her confidence. She'd never been one to give up. Not even when she'd found herself a prisoner in a cage. However, now that she'd gained her freedom, she realized she missed the walls of her cell. At least there she had shelter and food. Now, she had a giant spider crawling up her leg.

"Eeeeeeeek!" She screeched and leaped into the air, flailing and kicking her legs. The hairy eight-legged monster went flying, and before she could land, the stranger's hands were on her waist again, holding her aloft.

He stared at her, this tall and square man with the kind eyes. "You can't stay out here if you're going to scream every time you see a bug."

"It was huge!"

"It was the size of my thumb."

"You have big thumbs."

"You're coming with me."

He began to walk, still holding her aloft, taking a chance he wouldn't trip or run them both into a tree seeing as how he couldn't exactly see around her body or wings.

"Put me down."

"Better not. Who knows what you'll do if you encounter a centipede."

"Isn't that the worm thing with legs?" City girls didn't study the local fauna.

"I hope you're kidding."

Forget admitting she wasn't. "Put me down. You can't see anything."

"I'm using my outback senses to guide me."

"You are not Crocodile Dundee."

"Nope, that would be Uncle Kevyn. He was so pissed they went with that other fellow in the movie. He even shaved off his beard for the part."

"Interesting family."

"You have no idea, Angel. Now if I put you down, do you promise to not fly off?"

"Ha. Ha. So funny. I told you I can't fly."

"But you escaped out the window. I saw the broken glass."

"Yeah. And that's how I discovered it wasn't as easy as you'd think."

"I'm sure you'll get the hang of it with practice."

Practice? Was he insane? She ogled him, but only for a moment, as he set her down and moved around her body. She turned and saw him creeping toward the edge of the woods.

She followed him, but he whirled, grabbing her by the arms and forcing her to stand still. "Shh, Angel. You're making a ton of racket."

"I was walking."

"Exactly. We need to be quiet. There're people still in the building."

"Who are those people? And who are you for that matter?" she asked.

"Shoot, I guess we never did get properly introduced. Jebediah Peril Jones at your service. And you are?"

"Nevaeh."

"That's it?"

"That's all you need to know for now."

"A suspicious gal, probably smart, but not necessary with me. You'll soon see. I'm on your side."

"What side is that? Who are you? Why were you attacking the lab?"

"I'm what you might call special ops."

"For the government?"

"Not exactly. I do work for a higher authority, just not the one you think."

"But you're Australian?"

"Born and bred."

"I'm not," she admitted. "I emigrated here a few years ago from the USA for a fresh start." Only to discover a new location didn't always mean a fresh and better start. Not too many job opportunities for someone lacking a work visa.

"Wait here while I scout things out." He gestured her back before striding forth, a confident swagger to his step.

With each yard he put between them, her anxiety grew. Funny how the world didn't seem as daunting with him around.

You don't need a man. She could survive perfectly fine on her own.

Flutter. The feathers on her wings chose that moment to ruffle in a slight breeze as if mocking her.

Halfway across the cleared strip of land, another man came to meet Jebediah, the two of them stopping to converse. The distance should have been too great for her to hear anything, and yet...if she strained...

"...haven't found anything inside," said the stranger.

"Nothing in the woods either," Jebediah lied with ease, which made her wonder how much of what he'd told her was true.

"Guess Kole managed to destroy all the experiments. Probably best. Poor bastards. I can't imagine being the result of some science project."

Yeah, it wasn't easy.

"I'm sure not everything he created was shit." Did Jebediah suspect she listened? Was that why he lied?

"Only because you haven't seen the files yet. Did you know he was using humans to make his hybrid monsters?" the other man asked.

Probably because Dr. Guffo got tired of playing with animals.

Jebediah coughed. "Humans, eh. Wow. Shocking. So, what's the plan? When we moving out?"

"We've almost finished grabbing all the hard drives we could find. And the uncles have already carted away every single piece of paper in the place, plus all the fridges with samples. All that's left is the equipment, and there's too much of it to move. Shame, it would be worth a pretty penny on the black market."

"It's contaminated."

"Which is another reason why it's staying put. We're done here now. Ready to head out?"

Jebediah shook his head. "Not quite. I wanna do one last perimeter check. You know, in case we missed something."

"You gonna make us wait?" Groan. "Dude, I am dying for a beer and some food. I don't dare touch anything in there. Might wake up as a platypus."

"It would be an improvement." Jebediah ducked a

punch tossed by the other man and laughed. "You go ahead. I'll catch up."

"How? You gonna hop home like you did from the chopper crash?"

"I'll just use one of the parked cars. Shouldn't be too hard to find some keys."

Hot damn, she was an idiot. She'd forgotten all about the vehicles parked in the nearby barn, hidden from sight lest satellites passing overhead see them. Dr. Guffo had complained about the dust in the barn dirtying his leather seats.

A car meant escape.

Forget waiting for Jebediah, who walked toward the building, his voice growing fainter. She took off in the other direction, taking a longer, circuitous route that brought her out at the rear of the barn. Before she could enter, though, she heard voices heading her way.

Quick. She had to hide.

With no time to run back to the woods, she did the only thing she could. Jumped high enough to grab hold of a protruding ledge and hauled herself up, hoping no one would circle around and think to glance overheard.

She could have cursed when she heard Jebediah nearing the barn still yapping with that other man.

Sliding along the ledge, she peeked around the corner and saw her rescuer slap his friend on the back and say, "Smell you later." To which the fellow flashed him a finger —a rude one—then strode toward the main building, never once looking back.

She eased back around the corner and held herself still, hoping Jebediah would leave, too. Just because he'd helped her thus far didn't mean he had her best interests at heart. She waited. And waited.

EVE LANGLAIS

Wondered if he'd left.

Heard the crunch of gravel as instead he circled around the building. She held herself plastered against the barn.

Damned man must have eyes on top of his head because Jebediah said, "You can get down from there now, Angel. It's just the two of us."

She glanced down. "How did you know I was there?"

"Outback instinct. Climb down."

She knew a quicker way. She leapt and hoped she didn't crash.

4

His heart just about jumped out of his chest when Angel threw herself off the ledge.

She extended her wings, slowing her descent, but Jebediah exclaimed, "Jeezus, Angel."

The corner of her mouth quirked. "Worried I was going to splat?"

"Can you blame me? You're the one who said you couldn't use those wings. Turns out you just need some practice."

"I'd rather get rid of them," she grumbled.

"Don't be talking crazy. They're beautiful." Just like her. "Now come on inside the barn. I want to wait a few minutes for the others to leave before we follow."

"That guy you were talking to, he's one of your work buddies?"

"You could say that." Good thing he liked his family— most of the time—given they worked together a lot. At least in a fight he knew they'd have his back.

"Did you find some car keys?" she asked.

"How did you know..." He smiled. "Heard us chatting, did you?" He held up a few sets. "I grabbed a couple from the front reception. Apparently, they had to leave them at sign-in with their phones." He jangled the keys. "Shall we see which chariot awaits us?" The first fob he clicked flashed lights in the shadowy barn.

"Bingo," he crowed.

Except the car he found was a tiny thing, great on gas, not on space. It took only a second for him to realize—

"I don't fit." Her lips turned down, and her wings drooped.

"Let's see if there's something bigger." There was, a sporty utility that she couldn't sit in, but if he laid down the seats, she could technically ride on her stomach.

Her lips pursed into a moue of annoyance. "This is ridiculous. I can't even sit in a damned car. What's the point of going anywhere with you? I might as well stay here." She stalked out of the barn, and Jeb jogged after her.

"Don't get upset. Just because these vehicles aren't made for angels doesn't mean we can't get one custom fitted."

"Who the hell is going to know how to custom fit a car to this?" A single wing flicked open.

"I know people who can help."

"Except for the fact I don't want people to know about me."

"They won't judge you, I swear."

She glared.

Tell her about the shifter world. Explain she's not alone.

Tell a human that the world was more complex than she knew? Except she wasn't human anymore and probably never would be again. The wings weren't the only thing that set her apart he'd wager.

He opened his mouth to tell her when the ground

rumbled. A moment later the main building housing the lab collapsed in on itself.

"Get down," he shouted as the dust cloud from the explosion raced toward them.

She hit the ground a moment before him, face turned to the side, eyes squeezed shut, as the dust blanketed them both. Then another explosion made the world rumble as the barn they'd just emerged from exploded as well, spewing wood and debris.

In a few minutes, everything was quiet again except for the crackle of fire as flames licked the remains.

Smoke and detritus hung in the air, a choking miasma that brought forth a cough.

Getting to his feet, he then hauled Angel to hers and dragged her away from the twin infernos. On foot. The vehicles stored within now mangled heaps of junk.

His earpiece crackled. "Jeb, holy fuck. Brother, answer me." Rare for Jaycon to sound panicked.

He tapped to open his microphone. "Relax. I'm fine. But I lost my wheels."

"Da says we can't turn back on account the fire department and cops might be on their way. But Uncle K says there's a dirt bike by the guard shack about a mile down the road. Guess they were using it to get back and forth from the lab."

A bike? "That's fucking perfect," he exclaimed before shutting off the line of communication. To those who thought it odd he could do that, they'd obviously never had to listen to their uncle boinking a woman during a mission.

The grunts haunted for a long time. After that, all their communication equipment came with an on-and-off switch.

"What's perfect?" Angel grumbled as he kept them moving past the scene of destruction. "Who are you talking to? Have they been listening this entire time? Do they know about me?"

"Don't worry. No one knows you escaped." He planned to keep it that way until he could decipher the situation better. "As to how we'll travel, I've got something better than a car for us."

She, however, didn't see it the same way. "You want me to get on the back of that?"

That being the dirt bike he found stashed in the brush by the guardhouse.

"What's wrong? I think it's the ideal solution."

"Says the guy who gets the largest part of the seat. I'll be sitting practically on the fender. I'll fall off at the first bump we hit."

"Then I'd suggest you hold on tight, Angel. Or would you rather wait and talk to them?" He pointed in the distance where the faint glow of flashing lights lit the sky.

Her lips pressed into a line. "If I fall off…"

"You won't." But if she did, he'd volunteer to kiss her boo-boos better.

Naked.

Hmm. Better not say that out loud. She'd probably peck out his eyes.

He straddled the bike, and—despite her protests—she settled on it behind him. The weight of them both pushed down on the springs, but they just needed to make it to the nearest town to find a better set of wheels.

Her arms stretched around him, and he reveled in her touch and closeness, pervy as it sounded. He jammed his foot down and revved the gas, kick-starting it to life. Then he headed away from the lights, despite her screech.

"Where are you going? The road is over there."

"So are the cops," he shouted over his shoulder. "Don't worry. This baby is made to go off-road."

The bike flew over the rutted packed dirt, and he thanked the darkness that hid their dust trail. He didn't thank it so much when he hit a rather larger bump and the bike soared.

Angel squealed, and he heard a flap. The bike stayed suspended in the air, managing a long glide. *Thump.*

Cool. "Do that again?" he yelled as he hit another swell in the ground.

And so they traveled, her squeals transitioning from fearful to excited. Even laughter at times as the pair of them worked together, riding and soaring through the night.

When they finally found a town, she didn't want to go near it. So he compromised, leaving her on the outskirts while he filled the tank with petrol. When dawn hit, they ditched the bike and hiked on foot.

They were close to their destination. A place he'd not been to in years. Lots of years. But he was pleased to find it remained intact.

He swept an arm at the hiding spot he'd chosen for her and said, "Tada! Take a gander at your temporary new home."

She was less than impressed.

"A TREEHOUSE? You're putting me in a treehouse?" she exclaimed, eyeing the wooden structure tucked in the boughs of a massive tree.

"Not just any treehouse. The Jones clubhouse. Built by me and my brothers." Said with such pride.

She eyed it dubiously, and for several reasons. One, young boys didn't have any kind of degree in engineering, bringing its stability into question. Two, how old was it? Jebediah wasn't exactly a teenager any more.

Did they have termites in Australia? Even if they didn't, they did have giant, creepy crawly things that probably loved old abandoned treehouses.

"Am I supposed to be reassured by the fact a bunch of boys built the playhouse?"

"Clubhouse," he corrected.

"You do realize I can't live in a little box in a tree."

"It's not little. You can't really tell because of the branches and stuff, but it's actually quite large. Wraps around the tree and has a second loft level."

"So it's a fancy condo-type treehouse. I am greatly reassured." The words spoken with perhaps a teensy tiny bit of sarcasm and a full-on eye roll.

"It ain't fancy." He rubbed his chin, staring up at the planks peeking from the branches. "But it's big and solid. It's a good temporary measure until we figure out something more permanent for you."

The fact that he mentioned help in finding something more permanent reassured. And she was being a bit of a bitch. He was trying to help. The least she could do was not rag on him. "Thanks. I'm sure it will be fine." She'd try not to think of the spiders and snakes that might crawl over her when she fell asleep.

Studies said people swallowed an average of three arachnids a year. She said whoever ran those studies should be shot for causing many a sleepless night worrying about it.

"Shouldn't be anyone coming around either."

"Other than tigers looking for fresh meat," she muttered.

"No tigers around here. Only thing you got to worry about is a stray gang of vampire quokka."

"What?" she squeaked. "What are those?"

"Cat-sized marsupials. Cute little buggers until they go for your jugular. Don't worry, though. My brothers are pretty good about making sure they stay off our property."

"Your brothers are around here?" she asked, shooting a look over her shoulder. Because, of course, she imagined them sneaking up.

"Yes and no. We're on Jones land, and they do know about the treehouse seeing as how we all had a hand building it. Adding something was a rite of passage. I raised the roof and added the loft with Jaycon. Jeremy helped, too, on account he was tired of crouching."

"Are your brothers all giant like you?" Because Jebediah was a large man. Broad, so very broad. She'd felt that as they rode the bike, her arms wrapped around him tight, her face tucked into his back.

There was a certain relaxing aspect to hugging someone. Jebediah made her feel safe. Which, in turn, made her grateful.

And horny.

Given her recent escape, the very idea of sex should have repulsed her. While never molested while in captivity —mostly because of the strict rules separating subjects from possible contamination through intercourse—she'd been subjected to a dehumanization of her body. Given no privacy. At all. Which meant, while the guards didn't touch, they did leer. They also said things.

Although they didn't say them as often once she'd twisted and broken one of the guard's wrists. Despite her frail appearance, Nev was strong. Much stronger than a girl her size and physical condition should be. It frightened her to realize just how much she'd changed since her capture.

"Two of my brothers are bigger."

His reply to her question had her blinking. Bigger? "Are they as bossy?"

"Bossier," he said with a smile. A smile that melted a hardness inside her.

In that moment, she realized something. *I'm free.*

A smile tugged at her lips. He saw and grinned wider. So pleased with himself.

She tossed her hair. Freedom didn't mean she was going to sleep with him.

Even if he was adorable with those twinkling brown eyes and rakish smile.

She crossed her arms and shot a glance around the clearing by the tree. "I don't suppose in your renos on the treehouse you added indoor plumbing."

"No plumbing, or even a bucket. We mostly just peed out a window."

"You're kidding right?" Her nose wrinkled.

"It's a guy thing." He shrugged, a sheepish expression making him cuter.

"I don't think my aim is that good." Which meant she'd have to squat in the woods. Something she hated and the main reason, despite her tight funds, she hated sleeping outside.

Give her the city any day. Her ass preferred the cold plastic seat of a toilet.

"I'll get you a bucket and some organic decomposing loo paper to wipe yourself."

"You one of those save-the-environment types?"

"Everyone should be. We all have to do our part to maintain the health of our planet."

"I draw the line at spreading my number two in the garden," she remarked, heading for the trunk of the tree.

"Then you're safe. We don't garden. My da and uncles prefer to let their fruits and vegetables grow wild."

"What if they can't find what they need?"

"That's what trading is for."

She paused at the wooden ladder affixed to the tree with rope of all things. Not a single nail holding it in. "I am having a hard time reconciling mercenary Jebediah with farmer Jebediah."

"Just Jeb."

"Well, which one is it? Who is the true Jeb?" she asked as she looked at him. In the institute, when they escaped, he'd possessed a hard edge, a dangerous vibe. Now, however, he was playful, sexy. No hint of the mercenary from before.

"How about neither and both."

"Getting deep on me, are you?"

"I'd love to."

No mistaking the wink. It froze her. She hugged herself harder and fought two urges. One, to flee, run from the smoldering promise in his gaze, or two, move into him and see if he would burn on contact.

He retreated. "That might have been out of line considering what you've been through. Sorry."

She realized he was apologizing for flirting. For treating her normal. She reached out and placed her hand on his forearm, sucking in a breath at the tingle that went through her fingers.

She met his gaze, his serious gaze. "After all you've done, I should be more grateful. I'm sorry, too."

"Aren't we a pair, apologizing. Meanwhile, you're probably knackered. Let's take a peek inside and make sure you're the only guest of the place."

"Not reassuring, Jeb. Not one bit."

He grinned. "Would you rather I lied?" He popped out of sight before she could reply, moving quickly up the ladder rungs, the rope binding them to the tree holding. She noticed some appeared newer than others. Someone was maintaining it.

He hollered down. "Give me a second to check the place out."

"No problem. Take your time." Vanquish any eight-legged spiders related to Shelob—that giant beast from *Lord of the Rings*.

Leaning against the trunk of the tree, she kept scanning the shadows and between the foliage for signs of anyone coming. "How long do you figure I need to stay here?" Asked more to make conversation than in expectation of a real answer. There was a reason she needed to hide out in a treehouse. She couldn't be seen in regular society, which meant what for her future? Was she doomed to hiding in the woods in a kids' construction for the rest of her life?

He poked his head out of a window above her. "You can stay here as long as you need."

Disappointment welled because that wasn't the answer she wanted. "What I need is to find a way to become normal again."

"That might not be easy, Angel, but I've got a few ideas if you'll trust me a while longer."

Trust. People asked for it and expected it to come so easily. She'd learned that the words were easily given, but those who actually meant it? Rare. As in, she'd never found one yet. Daddy always promised when he sobered it would never happen again. The next bruise called him a liar.

The doctor said it wouldn't hurt. Two weeks and she'd be free. Another fib.

So many lies she'd heard in her lifetime. So many broken promises.

Yet... *He did come back like he said he would.*

But he also lied. Jebediah admitted he thought she'd be captured. Thus, in a sense, he'd betrayed her already.

Then saved her.

Did that mean she could trust him? What other choice did she have? At least he hadn't tried to shove her into a cage.

But he might. Especially if he finds someone who'll pay to have their own live angel. It was what her father would have done.

May his liver rot and his teeth fall out, that bastard.

She squinted up at the treehouse. "There's no way we can get running water or electricity?"

He poked his head out. "All clear. Come on up."

He kept watch on her as she grabbed hold of the wooden slats. She rose, worried as she neared the trap-door. However, it was bigger than expected, plenty of room to squeeze her wings through. Probably modified because of giant shoulders.

As she hauled herself through, his hands steadied her, gripping and hauling her upright. She stood inside the treehouse.

Stood with room to spare overhead. She peeked upward. "You weren't kidding. It's big."

From the ground, looking up, she'd not seen too much of it. The tree had grown around the structure, or they'd always camouflaged it well to start with. Whatever the case, inside was more than just a roughhewn wooden box in a tree.

The floor was smoothed and even varnished. The walls painted a rainbow of colors. She arched a brow. "It's colorful."

Jeb laughed as he ran a finger from a royal blue that smeared purple then turned into a bright red. "We didn't have money to waste as kids on things like paint. So we took what we could get. Stray paint cans and old brushes. Odds and ends we found abandoned." He pointed to the bits of engines and tools hanging from the walls. "Da was the one who brought wooden pallets back from work for us to use."

"This wasn't just built with discarded wood." She glanced upward at the branches that curved overhead, forming a brace for the actual roof lain over it. That kind of strategic growth took years.

"Da helped Jeremy, my oldest brother, start it. That was more than thirty years ago." His expression held the kind of fondness that spoke of happy memories. "That's where we marked the shit that happened to us."

She noted the far wall had notchings: names, lettered abbreviations, and a short form date.

Seeing Jeb's name, she traced it. "What's this one for?"

"Fighting off a dingo and getting the scar on my calf." He pointed to his leg.

"And that one?" She jabbed at another.

"When I became a man."

"You marked down the first time you had sex?" She made a face.

"Of course not. It was the first time I won a fight with one of my older brothers."

"Sounds like a violent family." She knew all about that. Sadly, hiding the booze didn't help.

"Kind of, but we don't do it out of malice. It's just how the Joneses are. Boisterous, as Aunt Zara likes to say."

There was a bit of furniture in the treehouse. A few wooden stools. A rocking chair. Even a table with initials carved in the surface.

The place appeared fairly clean. A little dusty. Nothing a good cleaning wouldn't fix.

Overhead, a suspended rope ladder led to a loft.

"You checked everywhere for critters, right?" she asked.

"It's clear."

"Where am I supposed to sleep?" Because nowhere did she spot a bed, and the floor didn't appeal.

"You might need a few things to make it comfortable."

"And where should I shop for them?" Her wings flapped.

He winked. "Don't worry. I've got you covered. Give me a few to get back to the house and round up some supplies for you."

She sighed. "I don't suppose those supplies will contain chocolate."

They did, plus blankets, pillows, and a whole bunch of other things to make the tree house more livable. Even bug spray, which he used to bomb the structure, sending things scurrying. Even she had to admit after he'd made a dozen trips the place seemed homey.

The rocking chair had a cushion and a blanket draped over the back in case she wanted to wrap herself. The table held a basket of fruit and a cooler bag with more food. He'd brought an inflatable mattress and layered blankets on it along with two fluffy pillows. He'd even thought to bring clothes and toiletries.

She almost burst into tears. Instead, she tore into the fresh loaf of bread and chugged the chocolate milk.

"Where did you get all this?" she asked as she lounged in the rocking chair, now backless when he realized her dilemma. She held on to the armrests and managed a soothing motion.

Nev popped some fresh goji berries into her mouth while Jeb finished tacking some screens over the windows, doing the work via the illumination provided by a solar-powered lantern.

"I filched some of it from the house. We had things stored in the attic. The rest I got in town."

"Didn't people ask why you were taking the stuff?"

He shook his head. "I made sure to sneak it out. Your secret is safe."

"But I'm not." Nev sighed as she halted the chair. "What am I going to do? I can't live in your clubhouse forever."

"What if I told you I might have access to an ancient herbal remedy that might help."

She eyed him askance. "An herbal remedy to cure mad scientist experimentation?" She snickered. "Sure, why not? What is it? Some kind of mushroom that will make me hallucinate I'm normal again?"

He turned from the window he'd finished with a grin. "Nothing so crazy. I promise you won't see smoking caterpillars or talking bunnies so long as Miranda isn't around."

"Who's Miranda?"

"A strange lady you'll hopefully never meet."

"About this drug that's not a drug that you want to give me. What's in it?"

"Can't tell you, secret family recipe." He pulled a packet from his pocket.

"Is this some kind of outback cure?"

"Yes."

"A cure for wings?"

"Think of it more as a cure for the strange things that sometimes happen to people."

"Should I be wondering why your ancestors had a cure for that?"

"Shouldn't we instead be thanking them?"

"Only if it works." She cocked her head. "How many people have died taking it?"

"None that I know of." He snapped his fingers. "Actually, not true. Great-uncle Marvin did die after using it."

"What?"

"Yeah. Great-aunt Vivienne murdered him for being a philanderer."

"You mean it wasn't the drug."

"No, but Uncle Marvin did take it, trying to help with another problem. He misread the labels."

She threw a berry at him. "You did that on purpose."

"You deserved it. Do you really think I'd give you something that might hurt you?" He sounded offended.

"No, I don't think you'd hurt me on purpose."

"Good, because now you're going to try some of it."

"If I wake up with panties around my ankles, I will hunt you down and remove your man parts."

His eyes widened. "Angel, if I ever do something so heinous, I'll remove them myself." He handed her the packet.

"What do I do with it?" she asked, eyeing it askance.

"You just need to inhale a bit."

"Snort it like coke?" She grimaced. "I don't do drugs."

"Think of this more as medicine."

"Not exactly selling it, Jeb. Medicine got me like this in the first place."

"Try it, Angel. Please."

After all he'd done for her, and her current lack of options, what did she have to lose?

She pulled out a pinch and held it to her nose as he watched avidly. She inhaled through her nostrils, feeling the powder tingle inside them.

Jeb stared.

"So, are they gone?" she drawled sarcastically, feeling the weight of her wings on her back.

"No. Maybe it wasn't enough. Jax said it didn't take much with Mari, but that isn't exactly an accurate measurement. Each case is different."

"Who is Mari?"

"My brother's girlfriend. She had a problem similar to yours."

"Someone grafted wings onto her, too?"

"Not exactly. She was—still is, actually—an ostrich slash dinosaur."

"A what?" Nev exclaimed. Surely he joked with her. His serious expression obviously a sham.

"It's a long story, which kind of ends in me finding you. I'll tell you about it sometime. First, let's try some more."

She did three more pinches before he rocked back on his heels, frowning.

"I thought for sure it would work. Maybe Jeremy gave me a shit batch."

"And who is Jeremy?"

"My brother. He's the one who mixes up the recipes."

"How many brothers do you have?"

"Five."

"Sisters?"

"None. Probably why our mum ran off and made us think she was dead."

That caused her to blink. "Say that again?"

Jeb shook his head. "It's not important. What is important is now that you're all settled in, we should talk about your experience. Maybe if I know more how you got your wings, I can find a way to help you hide them."

"I don't see how telling how I got them will help. It was stupid. I answered an ad in the paper. Medical tests for money."

"You agreed to this?"

"No," she hotly exclaimed. "I agreed to normal tests. The kind that leave me human and a few dollars richer. It seemed legit, but the Bunyip Institute conned me into becoming some test subject for a crazy doctor, and now I am a freak for life."

"So you know the people who were involved."

"Some, like Dr. Guffo. He was the one who suckered me in. Then when he had me locked in the lab, he used to be assisted by Monroe and Carlson."

"What about Kole? The guy who owned the place?"

She frowned. "Who?"

"Short fellow, mustache, evil."

"Him? He owned it?" She frowned. "Are you sure? Because I thought it was his wife's deal."

"Wife?" He repeated the word slowly. His brow creased. "Describe this wife to me."

"Auburn hair, much lighter and more golden than mine. She had this fetish for red. Always wore it: dress, pants, shirt, shoes. She never wore any other color. Which really made her stick out, especially beside her husband— that short, mustached fellow." He acted more like her servant, and yet they wore matching rings.

"Are you sure it was her husband?" Jeb appeared really stuck on that point.

She shrugged. "I only ever saw them together, and he called her dearest. Usually had his hand in the middle of her back when they walked and they both wore wedding bands."

"What was her name?"

Again, her shoulders lifted and fell. "Never heard it. Everyone always called her ma'am and just about fell on the floor kissing her butt when she came around."

"And she was in charge? Not Kole?"

"That's how it seemed. Don't get me wrong, the short fellow had some pretty big airs for a man his size, and people kissed his butt, too, but not like they did with her."

"Which makes no sense. How would she have gotten involved?"

Her turn to frown. "Who? Do you know that woman?"

"My brothers seem to think the woman you're describing is our mother."

She blinked. "Your mother. I thought you said she was dead."

"That's what we were led to believe. However, the woman we saw peeking out of the helicopter…" He paused. "Either that was Ma or she's got a twin."

"Given the freaky science stuff going on at the institute, I'd have gone with clone."

For some reason, this made his lips quirk. "Clone is a good guess, too."

"How is it you seem to know so much about this?" Why didn't he seem more freaked out?

"Told you before, I'm special ops."

"Which tells me nothing. Someone hired you."

"Not exactly. We got involved because of our brother. Kole took him. We wanted him back."

"So your raid of the institute was—"

"A rescue mission. For my brother and his chick."

"Where you happened to find me. And weren't all that surprised." The realization dawned slowly. "You were expecting to find something."

"Expecting it? Kind of. Seeing it…" Jeb shrugged. "I didn't realize the extent to which Kole was following in Mastermind's footsteps."

"Who?"

"No one you need to worry about."

She stood and paced, the socks on her feet a nice warm

touch. "I do worry, though. What's going to happen to me, Jeb?"

"Nothing is going to happen. I'll make sure of it."

She snorted. "How? You can't promise me safety. Look at me." She fluttered her wings. "I'm a freak. Maybe I should join a circus. Become part of their sideshow act."

"You are not a freak."

"You keep saying that, and yet, with these wings, where can I go?"

"You don't have to go anywhere. I'll take care of you."

She wanted to bask in the promise of those words. Believe that he would keep her safe. She knew better. Her hair flew as she shook her head. "I can't stay here forever. Just like you can't protect me forever. Eventually, someone will find out."

"You need to trust me, Angel. I can fix this."

"No. You can't. No one can. I'm screwed." Her inner fear emerged strident. What could she do?

The more she paced, the more agitated she became, her feathers rippling with her anxiety, her fingers tensing and elongating. Literally. She hid their length by balling them into fists. Just another freaky aspect to her change.

She might have flung herself out into the night, but Jeb grabbed hold of her, steadied her, and forced her to look at him.

"Don't you start with that woe-is-me shit now. You survived what they did to you. You're free now."

"Free? You call this free?" Her laughter was as bitter as her tears.

"It's a start. Baby steps, Angel. We need some time to figure this out."

"But…" Her lips trembled as the bleakness of her future loomed, overwhelming her strength.

"No buts. We'll find a way. Together." A promise accompanied by a dip of his head as he kissed her. Their lips touched, and something sparked between them; heat and awareness. Something that had her sucking in a breath even as she leaned closer.

His hands spanned her waist, tugging her close to the inferno of his body. Her mouth parted for the decadent slide of his tongue.

She ran her fingers through his coarse hair, the thickness of it like silk.

His lips feathered kisses along her jaw to the lobe of her ear.

He sucked it.

She almost hit the floor.

He sucked some more, finding a weak spot, exploiting it. Igniting all her senses. Making her yearn for more.

A cawing outside had her pulling away, the moment interrupted. For a moment, they stared at each other.

Her lips tingled.

She wanted to lean back in and finish what they began. Instead, she pushed away.

"It's getting late," she said, her voice high and unsteady.

He cleared his throat. "It is. I, uh, probably should go."

"Yeah, you should. I need to, um, wash my hair." Which, given she only had a bucket, was the lamest excuse ever.

"I'll be back in the morning. Hopefully with answers."

"Feel free to bring hedge clippers, too."

He looked so appalled a snicker actually slipped past her lips.

"Just kidding," Nev sang.

"Somehow I doubt that." His lips curved. "Sleep tight, Angel. See you in the morning."

He was really leaving.

Leaving her alone. Which was fine.

Totally fine.

I'm a big girl.

All alone. In the woods. She huddled under the blanket and tried to not imagine anything crawling underneath it, wishing she'd had the courage to ask him to stay.

I SHOULD HAVE STAYED.

Leaving Angel didn't sit well. Kind of like one of Da's meals when his uncle the chef wasn't around to feed them.

Given the frightened look in Nev's eyes, insisting he stay seemed pushy. Jeb needed to earn her trust, which wouldn't be easy because her incarceration had made her skittish. Understandably so. However, under that trepidation, he also saw courage. She'd have to be strong to survive what Kole had done to her.

Kole, not his mum. No way could his mother be party to this kind of atrocity.

A mother who left her sons could.

His mother was dead.

Nev was who he should be concentrating on. He needed to find a way to help her cultivate her courage while treading slowly and carefully so he wouldn't trigger her escape instinct. Else, he had no doubt she'd fly the nest he'd built her the first chance she got.

Worry about her was why he chose to sleep under the stars that night, out of immediate sight of the treehouse, yet close enough he could come to Nev's rescue if she needed him.

An hour into his watch came the first text message. His phone vibrated, and he lifted it to glance at the screen. Ah friggin' hell, a group text.

Jeremy: Where you at?

Jeb: Nice night to look at the stars.

Jaycon: Who you shagging?

Jeb: No one.

Jeremy: The code word for his hand.

Jaycon: He really should give it a nickname.

Jeb: I am not whacking off.

Jeremy: Then why did you take a comforter and pillow?

Stupid brothers. They'd noticed him pilfering some stuff after all.

Jeb: Nothing wrong with getting comfortable.

Jaycon: Okay, you lily-skinned sheila.

Jeb didn't reply to the insult. He was not soft. Angel's skin on the other hand…

He stared around the bole of the tree at the treehouse perched yonder. Built when the boys were young, their secret hideaway. A place to play, collaborate, drink… But not a permanent place for a lady.

What was he going to do with Angel? He'd really hoped the powder would work. The same recipe had done wonders with Mary-belle when she'd had that problem switching back and forth between her shapes. It even worked on ferals, shifters who'd lost their way and needed help regaining their human form.

But it didn't do a thing for Angel. Was it because she started out human? He needed to know more, maybe dig into some of his ancestors' notes at the house. But that meant leaving her alone.

Only for a few hours.

Surely, she'd be fine.

He gave one last peek before trekking the familiar path back to the house. The sprawling ranch had been in the family for several generations now and had grown from its original shack to a thing with numerous rooms, the better to accommodate a large family with lots of relatives always coming and going.

Given their recent mission, it was fuller than usual, with all his brothers in attendance, minus Jaxon. He'd lost his lady bird and gone looking for her.

With that exception, everyone else—Jones brothers, fathers, and uncles—were gathered around the massive kitchen table and island. They paid him no mind when he walked in. They were all more intent on seeing what Jaycon displayed on his laptop screen.

Squeezing between Uncles Kyle and Kevyn, Jeb peeked to see what held their interest.

A video.

A shaky video taken of the helicopter that had escaped with the woman in red.

The woman they suspected of being their mum.

No one said a word as they stared.

The clip ended.

"Rewind."

They watched again.

The only person not paying it much mind was their da. He puttered around the kitchen, doing dishes—which he hated—wiping off the counter—also hated—and doing a shit poor job of pretending disinterest.

So Jeb blurted the obvious. "How long have you known she was alive?" Silence descended as the Jones boys all eyed their father. The uncles, on the other hand, found the ceiling interesting. Kendrick even whistled not so innocently.

"Er. What you talking about? Just as surprised as—" Da lied, and his sons glared. Glared enough that their da sighed. "Ah fuck it. Yeah, I knew," he admitted.

"And you never thought to tell us?" barked Jeremy.

Da shrugged. "Tell you what? That she went a little crazy after Jaxon's birth? Decided being a mum wasn't her thing and took off to be with another man?"

"She left you for Kole?" The incredulity was seen on all their faces.

"But he's short."

"And pudgy."

"He's a feckin' koala. What can she possibly see in him?"

It was Uncle Kyle who replied. "Your mother wanted an easier life. One without diapers and holes in the walls." The brothers tended to be rambunctious when they played. Even their da and uncles sometimes contributed, their good-natured tussles not easy on flimsy plaster and furniture with spindly legs. "She wanted to be somewhere people served her instead of the other way around."

"But she's our ma. It's what ma's do." Jeremy kind of summed up their thoughts.

"Some mothers like caring for their family and stuff. Others…they find it too hard and—" Da made excuses.

Jaycon interrupted. "And some lack the balls to take responsibility and leave."

"I don't believe it." It was Jeb who shook his head. He wouldn't believe it of the woman who used to tuck him in at night and read him a story. "Kole must have done something. Blackmailed her. Threatened us."

"For over twenty years?" It was his father who pointed out the glaringly obvious fact.

However, something about it just didn't feel right. Surely there was more to it than that.

An argument ensued with some brothers insisting they needed to save Ma.

"She's obviously a prisoner."

"Being blackmailed."

"We should rescue her."

To the more pragmatic ones.

"She skipped out on us."

"We should get revenge."

Jeb might have jumped into the argument except he had something more on his mind than a woman who'd ignored her flesh and blood for decades.

"So that institute we rescued Jax and Mari from, what exactly were they doing there?" Jeb asked. "Did we find anything out? Crack the files on those hard drives yet?"

A negative shake of Jaycon's head preceded his reply. "They are locked tight. I'm working on it. It would have helped if we'd found some of the subjects alive. But other than Mari and Jaxon, they'd already evacuated the viable ones. Judging by the puddles of goop we found, they eliminated the rest with that gas before they totally demolished the building with a hidden bomb."

They didn't suspect at all about Angel. Jeb went to sigh, only to almost choke when Jaycon said, "But I think at least one of them might have escaped."

"Really?" Jeb said.

It was his older brother who explained. "I was watching the web for trigger words." Trigger words being sightings by the uninformed humans of possible shifters. "I saw something on a Twitter feed. Some bloke living out by the institute claims he saw a giant bird with wheels instead of legs go flying by last night."

Jeb did his best not to react. "Obviously drunk."

"Could be, but just in case, I think a few of us should head back out and see if we can track any scents. If some of those experiments did manage to get out, then we should capture them before anyone else does." The anyone else being humans, of course. "Who's in?"

Jakob and big Jackson—yet another brother spelled with a K instead of an X to fuck with people—immediately raised their hands.

Jeremy glanced at Jeb. "What about you?"

Leave now, with Angel hiding in a tree? The right thing was to say no. However, that would look suspicious. Not to mention, what kind of trail had he and his angel left during their mad flight from the institute?

"Totally in. As a matter of fact, how about I leave tonight." He just had to make one detour first.

7

SOMEONE IS WATCHING ME. A common occurrence when living in a cage. Except Nev had escaped the cage, so who stared?

She opened her eyes, and glowing yellow ones peeked back at her. It drew a scream.

A loud one as she scrambled to her feet, away from the intruder, her wings flapping in agitation.

The snake dropped to the floor, its thick shape undulating as it moved toward her.

"Oh hell no!" she yelled. Despite her fear, she dove forward and grabbed the snake behind the head like she'd seen on animal shows. The scaly skin repulsed her, and the serpent, unhappy with her handling, tried to lift its tail to coil around her.

Using her foot, she lifted the trap door and then thrust her arm through, giving one last squeak of terror as the thing hissed before falling to the ground. Probably plotting its revenge. She slammed the trapdoor shut and tried to catch her terrified breath.

"Angel!" Jeb called to her, and before she could reply,

his head popped through the trap door. The rest of him soon followed, and she couldn't help but throw herself at him, looking for the comfort he gave.

He caught and held her. "Your heart is pounding. Are you all right?"

"I'm fine," she muttered. "Just had to take care of a visitor."

He squeezed her. "Did Verm pay you a visit?"

"Verm?"

"Pet python. When he got too big for the tank in the house, Da had us put him outside."

"You knew there was a snake and didn't warn me?"

"I thought for sure he'd moved on by now."

She shoved away and hit him in the chest. Might as well hit a brick wall. "You jerk! I thought it was going to kill me."

"Who, Verm? I'm sure he just wanted to say hello."

She glared. "Not funny, Jeb."

"Does this mean you're not happy to see me?" He grinned.

And damn him, but she was happy to see him. "What are you doing here? It's the middle of the night. I thought you left." What did it say about her that she was glad he hadn't?

"I did leave, but I came back to tell you I've got to go away for a few days."

"What? Where? Why?" Add in a who and she'd sound like her third-grade teacher.

"Apparently, we didn't get away completely unseen. My brothers are heading out to see if they can find a trail. I'm going to get ahead of them and make sure there's none."

"You're leaving to protect me?" The sweetness of it restarted the flutter in her heart.

"I told you I'd keep you safe. But I didn't want you thinking I'd abandoned you." He held up his arm and showed her a sack dangling from his hand. "I brought some more food. Mostly canned stuffed. It should tide you over until I return."

"You won't abandon me?"

At the soft words, he reached out and ran a knuckle down her cheek. A tremor went through her.

"Never. I promise. I'll just be gone a few days. Think you can handle it?"

No. Yet that wasn't what she said. She nodded. "I don't have much of a choice, I guess."

He drew closer, the size of him overtaking the space, and yet she didn't mind. She drew comfort from it. He pulled her against him. "Stay hidden."

"What if someone finds me?"

"No one should. You're on Jones land. But if they do…" He dug into his pocket and drew out a phone. "I took one of the spare burners we keep at the house. I programmed my number into it. And the one for my brother, Jaycon. If you're in danger, you don't hesitate. You call him."

She took the phone and bit her lower lip. "Wouldn't it just be easier if I went away?"

He barked, "No. Because then I'd have to find you."

She raised her gaze to meet his. "And why would you do that?"

"Because."

Before she could reply that because wasn't an answer, his lips pressed against hers creating that same electrical sensation as before.

She sighed into his mouth, relaxing into the kiss, feeling her body respond in a way she never thought it would again.

She leaned into him, the feel of his hard body welcome against hers. The heat of the embrace warming all the cold parts, especially her jaded heart.

All too soon, and before she'd had enough, he pulled away. "I should get going."

She almost asked him to stay. Almost.

Instead, she hugged herself as he popped back out of the treehouse, leaving her alone.

All alone. *Now's my chance to go.*

Rather than escape, she lay down on her stomach in her nest of blankets and waited. And waited.

The next day, she explored her limited area. Ran into Verm again. When he hissed, she hissed back. But was it her, or did it smile?

That afternoon she caught a rodent trying to eat her crackers. She gave it to the snake for dinner. In return, Verm took care of the creature snuffling at the foot of the tree in the night. His bulging belly the next morning showed he'd made it into dinner.

It was quiet in the treehouse. A peaceful if wary existence. An even more precarious freedom.

But it was freedom. She saw no one else during her wait. Never thought she'd miss seeing other people. Eventually, the solitude sent her looking.

Following an overgrown path, she discovered a house at the end of it. A sprawling affair with the windows alight even late at night.

The scents that bombarded her—smoke, food cooking, exhaust—sent her scurrying for the wild safety of the woods.

Yet, day after day, when the witching hour hit, she crept back to peek. Wondering if Jeb had returned.

Hating herself for the weakness. Yet unable to stop the yearning.

It was three days before he returned. Three days of her wondering if he'd come back.

On the third evening, she heard it, music in the distance.

Despite the early evening hour, she crept out of her hiding spot, the darkness hiding her approach.

She came close enough to hear not only the strains of rock and roll but the ribald sound of laughter and conversation. A party.

Heading away from the lights in the yard, and the tables set with platters and bowls of food, Jeb.

He's back!

Quickly, she fled back to the treehouse and had barely made it inside when she heard someone approach. She peeked from the window to see who.

The familiar lanky walk and wide shoulders could only be one person. Jeb! He returned with a carefully balanced covered plate of food.

Freshly made food. She could smell something barbecued.

Her stomach gurgled, but she didn't rush down to greet him.

He'd been gone for so long. Without a call to the cell phone that died that morning. Enough time for her to second-guess everything.

Which might explain why, when he whistled, she muttered, "I am not a dog."

8

JEB SMILED AT HER REPLY. Because she was right. She was much cuter than any canine.

"I brought food." He held up the offering.

"Yes!" The happily hissed word preceded her head poking from a window where she'd loosened a screen, probably in case she needed a quick exit. She clambered out and perched on the sill.

But he didn't panic, not like the first time he'd seen her atop a ledge. She leaped, a graceful and petite thing, her shadowy wings easing her descent. He smiled in pleasure at the sight of her.

His very own angel.

What a pity he'd long ago lost his halo. But lucky for him, she didn't seem to mind.

"I brought you something." He held out the plate, and she dove on it.

"Ribs! Ooh potatoes," she exclaimed. She dug into the repast, humming happily.

Whereas he was happy just seeing her. The days he'd spent away, she'd been on his mind. Not just because he worried about her safety but because he couldn't forget the kiss they'd shared.

Emasculating in some respects, men weren't supposed to moon over kisses, and yet the memory of it was what kept him tracking and backtracking, looking for traces of their passage. Finding stray feathers and burning them. Scuffing out the tire marks. Pretending innocence when he ran into his brothers and said, "Nothing this way."

The good news was that, between the fire and the efforts to extinguish it, nothing remained of the secret lab. Nothing to link back to Angel.

So long as everyone, especially Kole, thought she was dead, the better.

In between bites of food, she asked, "How long are you going to keep me here?"

Funny how the word forever came to mind. Given she'd probably assume the worst and throw something at him if he said it, he instead stuck to, "I don't know. Until we can find a way to hide those wings, going out in public is obviously a no-no."

"I told you, pair of garden shears will remedy that problem."

"And I told you, no cutting."

She paused her eating to regard him. "Do you have some fetish for a woman with wings? Maybe some secret fantasy? Is that why you're so against me having them removed?"

"No matter how you got them, they are an intricate part of you now. What if they're connected to a major artery? Or you need them to live or something?" Not to mention they were beautiful. How could she think of amputating them?

"Beautiful?" she queried.

He blinked. "Did I say that out loud?"

"I heard it, didn't I? I don't know how you can think it's beautiful when they make me a freak."

"You are not a freak."

"Says the man who thinks I should remain hidden."

She had a point.

Tell her about shifters.

She'd never believe him.

I could show her. Show her my kanga side.

What if that made things worse? He'd heard stories. Horror stories of humans completely losing their shit at the news. According to Uncle Kevyn, the reason Boggy Joe never came to town was because his lady love killed herself once she found out she'd married a swamp beast.

Could the knowledge be the thing that put Nev over the edge? And what if her wings weren't permanent? She did start out as human.

"We're hiding you for your own protection."

"I know." Her shoulders slumped. "And I don't mean to sound ungrateful. It's just so boring out here all alone."

"I'm back now."

"For how long?"

Even he knew better than to promise anything. There were times he'd have to leave her. "What if I said I knew someone who might be able to help you? Someone who wouldn't turn you in or freak out because you are special?"

"Who?"

"A doctor."

She recoiled, and her wings lifted, peaked and ready for flight. "No doctors."

"I swear, Dr. Fleetwood would never hurt you."

"What kind of doctor is he?" she asked, suspiciously.

"Um." He hemmed.

She arched a brow. "Foot doctor? Maybe a butt one? Something completely useless to my case."

"Dr. Fleetwood isn't useless. *She's* a vet."

"A retired army doctor? That might work. They usually have experience amputating limbs and stemming blood flow," she mused aloud.

"Vet as in veterinarian."

"You want me to see an animal doctor?" At that, she laughed for the first time since he'd met her, a rich sound that vibrated through his body.

"She's got experience with your kind of condition."

"My kind of condition?" Her gaze narrowed. "What's that supposed to mean?"

Time to tell her. To let her know she wasn't alone. He opened his mouth, only to shut it as his phone went off in his pocket.

Bzzz. Bzzz. Bzzz. Which was the angry bumblebee that meant family emergency. Everyone gather at the house.

"Shit, I gotta go. Family needs me for something."

She glared. "Must be nice to not always be alone."

"You have me."

"Only in your spare time," she grumbled.

"Why, Angel, is this your way of saying you miss me?" He grinned.

Her scowl deepened. "I don't need you."

Which they both knew was a lie. "I know you hate hiding, but it's for your own safety. Which is why I think you should give the doctor a chance."

"Whatever." She turned her back on him, her wings drooping as she went back to her hidey-hole.

A hole he'd have to get her out of. She was right. It

wasn't fair. She deserved to have a life that didn't involve hiding.

And he'd get started on that as soon as he found out what the emergency was.

Turned out it was less emergency and more like surprise.

When Jeb got back to the house, he noticed right away the strange sedan parked outside. And the scent... Stranger danger.

Inside, he found everyone gathered in the living room. Jones family on one side. Man with a brush cut wearing a tan shirt and camo pants across from them.

However, it was what he said that made them all shut up.

All the boys blinked as they digested his words. It was so quiet you could have heard a wallaby fart—which he might add was louder than folks expected. But not as smelly as Uncle Klaus after chili night.

The FUC agent, a veritable croc named Viktor, stared back at them. He didn't seem at all perturbed by the fact the Joneses outnumbered him.

"I think we heard you wrong," Da said. "Because I could have sworn you asked the boys to become legal FUC agents."

Viktor nodded. "I did."

At that, the silence broke and laughter washed over the room, boisterous chuckles because, if there was one thing the Jones brothers weren't, it was blokes who worked for legal agencies. Not anymore at any rate. They'd done their stint for the Shifter Special Forces. Discovered they didn't like taking orders and went their merry way. They still did occasional missions for various agencies, but on their terms. They didn't need a badge or special agent status to act. The raid on Kole's lab was proof of that.

"He's pulling our fuckin' legs," snorted Jackson.

"Never knew the leather-skins had a sense of humor," added Keith.

"This is not a joke." The FUC agent fixed them with a yellow-eyed stare. "We find ourselves understaffed in this part of the world at the moment. Probably by design, given Kole's unsanctioned activities. We are in need of qualified young men and women who aren't afraid of danger or getting their hands dirty."

"We ain't afraid of nothing," boasted Jakob. "But I don't know if I'd call us qualified. At least not when it comes to doing things legal like."

"Which is actually what makes you ideal. We need people familiar with the land who can blend in. Shifters like you, with a keen sense of observation." Viktor's hand shot out, and he yanked Kevyn close, Jeb's uncle's fingers still wrapped around a wallet. Pickpocketing was a specialty of his.

The croc was fast, though.

"And just why should we help you?" Da asked, leaning forward.

"You'll be paid, for one. FUC agents are well remunerated, and we offer an extensive benefit package."

"We get paid well already," Jeremy said. The Jones brothers had long been advocates and players on the Australian black market. Their special powdered blend of various handed-down recipes—curing things like baldness, moon madness, irritable bowel, and more—fetched a pretty penny since they kept the stock low and rare. "And we have all the motorized toys a boy could want." Plus some that went kaboom.

"We are well aware of your activities," Viktor replied. "As well as the warrants out for your arrest." He slapped a thick file on the table.

"Warrants with no name?" teased Jaycon, who was very good at obscuring their trail.

"What if I said I could wipe those charges clean?"

"Tempting, but you're talking about answering to someone outside the family." Jakob grimaced. "I don't know if I want to be answering to some bloke who sits in an office all day."

"What I think the boys are saying is no." Da shook his head. "Nice offer but I think we'll stick to our own thing."

"Are you sure? Because there is one more thing you might be interested in." Viktor slid one last envelope onto the table. From within spilled satellite images.

Images of their missing mother, obviously taken over a period of time because there was a young girl with her. A girl who got older as the photos progressed.

"Is that…"

"Your mother and sister?"

"Sister!" Jakob's squeak covered all their surprise.

"Yes, sister. Half of a set actually. There's a boy too. I have pictures. Information if you're interested." The croc leaned back with a smug smile as they stared a while longer.

It was Jeremy, his expression shocked, who finally mumbled. "We're in. But with one condition."

The boys all grinned as Da gave his terms. Viktor agreed to them all then stood to leave.

"Your badges will arrive by special post shortly. Welcome aboard, agents."

"License to FUC" More than one Jones snickered.

Pausing in the doorway, Viktor fixed Jeb with a yellow

stare. "By the way, given our agreement, the agency will overlook the fact you hid one of Kole's test subjects."

Jeb's blood ran cold as his dad replied, "Don't know what you're talking about."

Viktor smiled. "Perhaps you don't, but your son does. As we speak, Agent Chase and my wife, Renee, are being dispatched to apprehend the fugitive in the woods."

Jeb couldn't contain himself. He stepped forward, mouth open, only to have his uncle slap a hand over his mouth and draw him away. "Shut up, you moron."

He glared at his uncle.

"Don't give me those baby 'roo eyes. Your girl is safe."

Jeb gaped. "How did you know about Angel?"

Da snorted. "As if you could keep it secret."

"Soon as the car pulled onto the property, I sent Kary to get her to safety," Uncle Kevyn announced.

Which didn't reassure. Angel wouldn't trust his uncle to protect her.

She needs me.

And he wasn't about to break his promise to her.

9

NEV HEARD the bright chatter long before anyone came into view.

Had Jeb changed his mind? Had he told someone about her? Either way, didn't matter. She wasn't about to get captured, which was why she exited through an escape hatch in the roof of the treehouse and perched herself in the next tree over, a vulture ready to pounce if needed.

Perhaps the voice belonged to the animal doctor Jeb had mentioned.

However, if that were the case, why didn't he accompany them? And who was the other woman walking beside her?

The women stopped in the clearing by the tree. One, a curvy blonde with her hair in a ponytail wearing the shortest, most disreputable jean shorts ever and a plaid blouse tied off at her midriff. Her companion, a slender redhead, wore attire more appropriate for trekking, finished with solid boots.

"Well, smack me with a carrot and call it foreplay,"

exclaimed the blonde. "It's an honest-to-goodness tree-house. How adorable." She clapped in apparent delight.

The other woman, with fiery locks much longer than Nev's, cocked her head. "That's a house? Why would someone choose to live in a tree?"

Because trees were nice. Duh.

"I think it's cute. Think she knows we're here?"

"Probably. You talk a lot."

And they both apparently knew of Nev's presence. Who were they?

"Chase says I talk so much on account I don't get enough exercise, so to work off excess energy, I run my mouth a mile a minute."

The redhead shook her head. "I think I'd kill you if I lived with you. Viktor doesn't talk much."

"That's because he's the strong, silent type. Like my honey bear."

Odd conversation, especially given they made no attempt to hide their presence.

"I wonder why the girl hasn't come out yet. Yoo hoo," yodeled the blonde.

"She's probably scared," said the other woman.

"Scared of us? That's silly. Don't you worry, honey. We won't hurt you. We just want to talk."

"Lying isn't nice," stated the other. "You know our orders are to bring her in."

"Which might be a tad difficult now that you've told her." The blonde rolled her eyes.

"We'll explain it's for her own good."

Not Nev's good. Nev didn't care what kind of spin they put on it. She wasn't letting anyone lock her up again.

However, how to escape?

Verm took that moment to slither down from a tree

behind the women. While they had an understanding, these newcomers didn't, thus Verm had no problem wrapping himself around the ankles of the blonde.

She peeked down and said, "Wouldn't you make a nice purse."

Purse? While Nev and the snake might have gotten off on the wrong foot, he didn't deserve skinning. About to slide down the tree to save the snake, she paused because something odd was happening. The curvy blonde appeared to be getting hairier.

And bigger.

With ears.

Great big floppy ones. But it was the fangs that made Nev exclaim, "What the fuck, doc?"

And that was when shit hit the fan. Or, in this case, the bush.

Bodies suddenly appeared through the trees, sporting rifles with red laser sights.

There were shouts, too.

"Get the giant rabbit."

Except the giant rabbit wouldn't stay still. Probably a good plan. No one had spotted her yet, but it wouldn't be long before someone noticed the bird woman in the tree.

Nev scrambled over branches, only to squeak as a head sporting gray hair that matched a beard appeared in front of her.

"There you are! You need to come with me."

"Oh no, I don't," she growled, the darkness pulsing behind her eyes.

Something pricked her in the ass.

Darted.

It was the opening the darkness needed.

The fury inside her breast broke free.

❧ 10 ❧

RACING ALONG THE PATH, Jeb heard a high-pitched shriek before he saw anything.

Ah shit.

He tore at his shirt but didn't have time to stop and take off his pants or shoes.

In short order, he'd ripped through his clothes and his 'roo popped through. Only one thing drove him as he hopped away from the ranch: Angel.

She needed him.

She trusted him.

And she'd think he'd betrayed her when FUC showed up to take her prisoner.

Before he'd even reached the treehouse, he heard the sounds of battle. Many more than the two agents Viktor claimed he'd sent.

He leapt harder and faster, emerging onto a scene of chaos. It took a moment to grasp what he saw.

A giant bunny, with even bigger saber teeth, swung someone in a tan camouflage outfit around and around,

85

using the body to knock down other uniformed men with guns. Not real guns, he noted, but tranquilizers.

An enormous red fox snarled and snapped at a group of men herding her with cattle prods, the electrified tip drawing a yelp.

That yelp was met with a roar at Jeb's back, but he didn't have time to turn around.

He dove into the fray, fists flying, his hind quarters bunching as he leapt and twisted, keeping out of reach of the tan-clad folk while knocking them down.

The entire time he kept an eye open for Angel. Not easy given the tree had a bole wider than him and all his brothers. They'd chosen a sturdy one to build in.

He kept trying to make his way to the other side where he could hear the shrieks and screams of men being hurt.

When he finally did round the corner, he saw the wings first, spread wide, the tips of them razor sharp and edged in crimson.

Uncle Kary yelled, "Why didn't anyone tell me you found a harpy?"

Harpy? This graceful angel was more like a Valkyrie, leaping into the air, spinning and taking out the mini army arrayed against them.

Jeb hopped into the fray, punching left and right, pummeling when he saw his angel fall out of the sky, her body covered in tufts, the drugs overwhelming her.

Immediately, men tried to drag her away.

Uncle Kary punched one of them out. Jeb took care of the others. And there weren't any to take their place.

The ruckus finally died down, the area littered in groaning bodies. Some still ones, too. Jeb stood over Angel's sleeping form, fists raised, and while a kanga didn't usually bare teeth, he did even as the giant killer bunny hopped into view and turned into an attractive naked woman.

The FUC agent approached, hands outstretched. "I'm not your enemy."

Uncle Kary answered for him. "And yet you led them right to the girl."

"We don't want to hurt her," Miranda said, having swapped out of her bunny shape. "But we can't let the humans see her, either. Let her come with us. We'll keep her safe."

Jeb switched back to human so he could bark, "Safe? You want to lock her in a cage. She doesn't deserve it. She didn't do nothin' wrong."

"No, she didn't, and yet even you have to see we can't let her run around with those wings. Sorry." Miranda shrugged.

"I know we can't let anyone see her." And Nev knew, too. However, if he let her go, she'd never forgive him. "Give me a chance to try something."

Miranda arched a brow. "You think you can fix this?"

"Not me. But I know someone who might be able to."

The red fox, who'd turned into a lovely woman, draped herself around the knobby croc that had joined the fight and added her two cents. "Oh, give the man a chance. The same way you all gave me a chance after what Mastermind did."

"You're different, Renee." Miranda turned her gaze. "For one thing, you can hide what you are."

"What if I could hide her, too?" Jeb said.

"Hide those wings?" Miranda shook her head. "We both know you can't, and the council is expecting us to bring her in."

"I can't let you do that. She's a person. A victim." An angel. "She deserves a chance."

Miranda pursed her lips. "Maybe our target fled before we got here."

The croc snapped its jaw.

Renee tapped it on the snout. "Don't you dare grumble. It's the right thing to do."

Miranda wagged a finger. "You're getting your chance, hoppy man. I'll see what I can do about stalling the search for her. But you better find a solution to her wings. You know the council won't hesitate to terminate her if they think she's a danger."

"I'll fix this."

Somehow.

11

THE CUSHIONING FABRIC under her cheek vibrated, and yet Nev was comforted by the scent. The folded jacket exuded a musky aroma she associated with Jeb. It also smelled like diesel.

Or did that come from the tarp draped over her head?

Panic momentarily clawed at her, and she took some heaving breaths before freaking out.

The good news: she was alive, seemed to be unharmed, and was not tied down. The bad news? Judging by the jostling and engine noise, she was on the move in the back of a truck.

Whose truck? Last she recalled, she was under attack. Her body a pincushion for tufted missiles. Drugged!

Hello, familiar cottony mouth and cloudy head. It explained the hallucinations of a giant bunny, a car-sized fox, and a kangaroo with Jeb's eyes.

Drugs were never a good thing. Especially the kind that knocked you out. It meant that, despite the coat pillowing her cheek, she was probably in deep shit.

It was from one of her drugged episodes she woke to wings.

Currently she didn't appear to have any extra body parts, but that could change. Kidnapping never turned out well for women.

If this were an abduction, then the first thing she needed to do was find a way to escape, which might prove easier than expected given they'd foolishly just laid her in the back of the truck. Probably thought she'd sleep longer. Little did they know the experiments on her in the institute made her resistant to many narcotics and improved her recovery time.

She sat up, flinging back the tarp, sucking deep lungfuls of air, free of the dust they left in their wake. Despite the flying scenery, she was ready to throw herself out and hope she could glide to safety rather than crash and deal with road burn. A good, if possibly painful, plan that she held off implementing when she noted the back of the driver's head.

I know who that skull belongs to.

"Jeb?" Then more loudly. "Jeb!"

A quick glance over his shoulder netted her a wide grin and twinkling eyes. "Angel!" he exclaimed. "Hold on a second." He pulled over to the side of the road, the wheels barely stopped when he'd swung himself out of the truck, oblivious to the stinging dust. He leaned against the bed, arms casually crossed, still wearing the smile. "Wondered when you'd wake. Those bastards in the woods shot you up pretty good with tranqs."

"You were there?"

"I was. Arrived a bit late to the party but in time to make sure you didn't wake up with strangers."

"Who were those men who attacked? What happened

after I blacked out?" Because she wasn't about to admit to her cartoonish hallucinations. Giant bunnies with teeth, indeed.

"No idea who they were. I didn't stick around long enough to question them, but from the texts my brothers sent, it is starting to look like the institute was trying to get you back."

She shuddered. "Glad they failed. I guess when those women couldn't catch me they called in reinforcements."

"You mean Miranda and Renee? They don't work for Kole."

He knew them? "Are you sure? They wanted to take me away."

"Yeah, they snuck up on you while I was talking to Viktor. You don't have to worry about them anymore."

"Are they dead?"

A laugh escaped him. "Far from it. But they did agree to let me try and get you fixed first."

"Fixed as in my wings."

He nodded. "Yeppers. That's why we're on the road. Gonna take you to see that vet friend I was telling you about."

Ah yes, the animal doctor. "I still don't see what she can do for me. No one can help me."

"Already calling it a day?" He dangled his arms over the bed of the truck as he shook his head. "Where's that fighting spirit of yours? Don't give up, Angel."

"Easy for you to say. You're not the one who's half animal, half human."

"Says who?" He winked. "Could be there's more to me than meets the eye."

"If this is a boast about the snake in your pants, save it. I am not feeling sexy right now," she grumbled.

He snickered. "Gotta say, chewing the fat is never boring with you, Angel. Pity we've got to save it for later. We've still got a fair distance to go before nightfall."

The implication being they couldn't talk while they traveled. "Let me guess, I have to stay in the back."

"We could try you in the front, but I didn't think we were yet at a spot in our relationship where you wanted to lie sideways with your face in my lap."

Her cheeks flamed. "I am not that type of girl."

"I meant it more because the seat doesn't have room for you to sit properly with your wings."

She peered through the window to the cramped front seat. "Oh." Now she felt dumb.

"Sorry I didn't have a better vehicle to transport you in. I've got my brothers working on a solution so you can ride properly."

"But until then, I get to ride in the back," she said with a sigh.

"Look on the bright side, Angel. You get plenty of space to stretch out and fresh air."

"It's a dusty dirt road," Nev remarked.

He scratched at his scalp. "Yeah, so long as we're moving it's not too bad. However, you might want to stay under the tarp for parts of it."

"For breathability or to stay out of sight?"

"A little bit of both."

"Still open to using those shears," she grumbled.

He reached in and yanked her forward, his big hand cupping the back of her head. "No cutting. We'll find a way. Promise." Words he sealed with a kiss, which was becoming a habit of his. One she didn't mind since it warmed her insides and curled her toes. It almost managed to make her feel normal. Until she hid under the heavy canvas, her shirt—more like his shirt, a button up plaid worn backwards—pulled over her mouth and nose as they bumped along the rutted track he called a road.

On their way to an animal doctor.

Sigh.

Still, it was better than a cage.

However, her trepidation must have been why the rage bubbled inside when the truck finally came to a stop and she heard Jeb saying, "Hold on a second while I explain to Maisy about you."

Maisy? They were on a first-name basis? What happened to calling her a doctor?

Nev leaned up enough to peer through the window and thus saw the front door of the ranch-style home open and a woman with long ebony locks, a dark complexion, and a curvy figure built to make men ogle come running out.

The squealed, "Jebby!" was followed by a leap as the woman wrapped herself around him and then planted a smooch on his lips.

Things kind of turned a deep purple at that point.

A SHRIEK FILLED THE AIR, and Jeb gaped as Angel, her eyes glowing, her features drawn and stark, hit the ground behind Maisy with her wings extended. The keening cry emerged from lips pulled over teeth that appeared a little sharper than usual. She looked like a wild creature with the tendrils of her hair writhing as if caught in a static storm.

The claws at the ends of Nev's fingers were new. As was the evidence of her strength. She tore Maisy off him and tossed her a fair distance.

Luckily, Maisy had dealt with angry critters before and landed on her feet. Cats always did. However, being graceful of foot—and paw—didn't mean Maisy took the manhandling well.

A feline hiss emerged from Maisy. "Whoa, sister. What's got your knickers in a twist?"

Angel replied with another keening cry and took a step forward.

Given she wore a murderous expression—which, being

a man of experience, he'd seen many times before—Jeb quickly thrust himself between the two women.

"Calm down, Angel. You don't want to hurt Maisy."

The growl from her lips said otherwise.

"Bring it. I am not afraid of your jealous girlfriend." Maisy didn't help the situation, but she did clarify it for him.

Could she be right? Was his angel feeling a little possessive?

"Angel," he crooned. "You can calm down. Maisy and I are just friends."

"Hands off," Nev snarled, trying to reach around him. "Mine."

"You can have him," Maisy declared with a snort. "You can have all the Jones brothers for all I care."

Someone still held some bitterness over the way things had ended with a certain brother of Jeb's.

"Maisy and I are just friends," he reiterated. "You can put away the claws."

The declaration did little to quell Angel's chest-heaving agitation.

Jeb moved closer to her, hands out to his sides, his voice soothing. "It's okay, Angel. No one here is gonna hurt you."

"Speak for yourself," Maisy muttered.

Nev growled.

He shot Maisy a look over his shoulder. "Could you please not help for a second?"

"I am not the one who called out of the blue and said you needed my help."

"It's not for me. Nev is the one who needs it."

Maisy's full lips curled, and her dark eyes flashed. "I don't provide anger management treatment. Whoever is in charge of her flock should take her under their wing and teach her some manners."

"She has no flock," he said, watching Nev, who paced, the feathers on her wings rippling, her body taut. A new side to her. A fighter. "She's human."

Those words froze Nev, who pivoted to stare at him. "No, I'm not. I'm a monster." In an instant, she deflated. Her wingtips drooped, her fingers went back to normal, and her violet eyes went from fiercely glowing to a deep abyss of despair.

"Angel," he cried out, reaching for her, only to have her dance away from his grasp.

Before he could say anything else—re: put his damned foot in his mouth even worse—Maisy darted around him to confront Nev. "Nonsense. You're no more a monster than I am."

A brow arched in time with a wing as Nev replied, "In case you hadn't noticed, I have wings."

"Gorgeous ones, too. Kind of jealous, actually."

The reply slammed Nev's mouth shut, and she watched rather than acted as Maisy circled around her.

Since there was no blood being shed—for the moment —Jeb held his body and tongue still.

Maisy paused at her back. "Fascinating."

"Says someone who wasn't part of a science experiment," Nev grumbled. She shot him a look. "I thought you said she could help me. Did you tell her anything about me?"

"Uh, not exactly. In case someone was listening, I thought it best to keep the conversation brief."

"What is the story?" Maisy asked.

Nev's lips flattened, but she gave a summary. "Volunteered for some medical experiments. Turned out they were looking for people who wouldn't be missed so they could pull some Frankenstein shit."

"Before these experiments, I take it you had no unusual health issues. No growths? Strange rashes? Odd dreams?" At each query, Angel shook her head and snorted at the last.

"Do dreams of killing the doctors count?"

Maisy's lips curved into a smile. "I'd say those were normal given what they did to you. Speaking of which, were the wings grafted, or did they grow out of your back?"

Nev blinked. "Does the how really matter?"

"Actually, it does, because we can't exactly treat the problem if I don't know how they got there."

"I assume they sewed them on somehow." Nev shrugged. "I don't really know. One day I was normal and human, the next I woke up face down on a gurney with wings on my back."

Having not heard this part of her story before, Jeb could barely contain his shock. He couldn't even imagine. How hard it must have been for her. He'd known from birth about his 'roo abilities. Reveled in them even. But to suddenly be given no choice…

"May I touch your wings?" Maisy asked.

For some reason Nev chose to glance at him, her eyes asking what she should reply.

He nodded. "She won't hurt you, Angel."

"She's a doctor. Like *them*." Said with a hint of disdain.

"I would never do something like this. I swore to heal, not hurt," Maisy hotly declared.

It was the right thing to say. Nev bit her lower lip but nodded. "Go ahead. Touch them."

"Thank you." Maisy circled to her back, ignoring Nev's

stiff posture as she ran her hand down the wings, tracing the edge, rubbing the feathers, smartly not making mention of the blood crusting a few of them. She even slid her fingers in the gap on Angel's shirt—one of his, ripped up the back and then draped on and tied at the waist.

As Maisy explored, she spoke her findings aloud. "No signs of scar tissue. Firm cartilage. Proper bone structure. A fine layer of feathers."

"What did you expect?" he asked.

"I wondered if they were real. If they'd grafted, then there was a possibility they used engineered wings."

"Is that even possible?" he exclaimed.

"Cyborgs aren't just in movies anymore," was Maisy's reply.

"I'm not a robot," Nev hotly declared.

"No, you're not." Maisy stepped away from Nev. "You are very much real. And so are these wings. I don't think they sewed them on, but I'll be better able to tell once we get you inside with that shirt off. Let me ask you, how much did you weigh before and after the procedure?"

"I weigh less now," Nev stated, staring straight ahead.

"Were you overweight before?"

"No."

"Interesting. They did something then to reduce your overall weight, probably to ensure the wings could support you."

"Meaning?" Jeb asked.

"Could be they managed to lighten her bones. Again, I'll need to do a proper exam to be sure."

"Why does it matter if I'm lighter than before?" Nev snapped.

"The more I know, the better I can help you. Now, I've

seen you moving them. Given your superhero leap from the truck, I know you can glide. Can you fly?"

A moue of annoyance creased Nev's face. "No."

Jeb didn't mention her attempt out the window that she claimed ended in failure.

"At a glance, your body seems healthy. Your cognitive skills appear sharp. So, what's the problem?"

Nev snorted, and her wings fluttered. "In case you didn't notice, big wings at my back."

"Put them away."

"Where? In my freaking purse?"

"Pull them back into your body."

For a moment, Nev blinked. Then she snapped, "I don't want them in my body. Or outside it for that matter. I want them gone." Nev stomped away from Maisy and headed to the truck. "This is a waste of time. She can't help me. No one can."

Maisy shot him a look. "Is she always this melo-dramatic?"

"It's been a tough few months for her."

"And they will be tougher if she keeps playing the woe-is-me victim."

"I can hear you," Nev shouted.

"Good. Then you'll hear me when I say you can stop being a drama queen. Get your butt into the house."

"Why?" Nev whirled, arms folded over her chest. "You can't help me."

"Says you. I said no such thing."

"So you can help me?"

"Never said that either. I don't know what I can do for you. Not until I run some more tests."

"What if I don't want to do tests? What if I want to go

home?" Nev pouted, and yet Jeb didn't get frustrated because he understood why she did it.

He held up a finger to Maisy and mouthed, "give me a minute." Maisy nodded and angled her head to the house before leaving him alone with his angel.

He sauntered over to the truck where she sat in the back, ass parked on the lip, wings hanging over the edge.

"It's okay to be scared, Angel," he said.

She glared down at him. "I'm not scared. We're wasting time. She can't help me."

"You haven't even given her a chance."

"A chance to do what? Poke and gawk at the freak."

"If she studies you—"

"What can she do?" Nev interrupted. "What can anyone do?"

"Remember that powder I made you try?"

"You mean that placebo shit that did nothing," was her bitter reply.

"Maisy knows more versions of it. Stronger ones."

"More drugs." Said with a sneer. "I doubt there is a pill or powder or potion that can fix the damage caused by a mad scientist."

"Then what do you have to lose trying?"

The word emerged, soft and gut wrenching. "Hope."

"Ah, Angel." He vaulted into the bed of the truck so he could kneel in front of her. He caught her hands in his, massaging the chilled flesh, catching her gaze with his own. "Don't give up."

"I'm not. It's just..." She paused and dropped her gaze to their hands. "How can I ever live a normal life with these things? I'll never find happiness."

"I wouldn't wager on that." *I'll make you happy.* If he

had to find them a remote mountain location where she could live freely in the open, he'd do it.

Her lips trembled as she admitted, "I'm scared, Jeb."

"Don't be. I won't let anyone hurt you." He gave her a soft kiss, one meant to encourage and show strength. She softened against his mouth and melted into him. The kiss lasted but a moment, and then her forehead pressed against his.

"Do we have to go inside? Can't we go back to the treehouse instead?"

"You need to do this, Angel."

She sighed. "Fine. Let's see what your animal doctor can do. But I swear, if she tries to kiss you again, I won't be responsible for my actions."

"Jealous, Angel?" he teased.

"I don't share," was her retort as she swung her legs over the side and vaulted off.

He stood and watched her stalk to the house.

Neither do I, Angel.

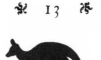

Entering the house, Nev didn't allow herself to be fooled by the cheery colors or the fresh scent of flowers.

That woman, humming in the kitchen as she put a kettle on the stove, was a doctor.

The enemy.

There was only one thing doctors wanted to do.

Hurt. Use. Humiliate. Okay, so that was three, but it wasn't hard to spot a theme.

Nev turned her gaze left and right, looking for the medical equipment. The bed with straps. The syringes. She saw instead a wicker frame couch with thick pillows. A woven, rag-strip rug in a mosaic of colors. A battered coffee table strewn with remotes and magazines.

"I thought you were a veterinarian," she said, seeing no signs of cages. Heck, other than a faint aroma of cat—an odor that reminded her of poor dead Rory—she smelled no animals at all.

"I am a vet, but I don't practice inside. I have a barn at the back for that. Although, most of the time, I go to the animals in need. Easier than transporting a sick bull or a lost joey whose mother might be looking for them."

"So we need to go to the barn then?" Nev tried to sound brave about it, the idea of putting herself at the mercy of a doctor, even an animal one, not sitting easy with her.

A gusty laugh emerged from Maisy. "No barn for you. That's for wild creatures. Of which you're not."

The answer took Nev by surprise, and she whirled to stare at Maisy. The woman set a mug on the counter and pointed to it.

"Come sit over here. I brewed you some tea."

"Gonna knock me out?"

Jeb exclaimed. "Angel! Maisy would never—"

"Oh hush, Jeb. The girl has a right to be suspicious. If she were a rampaging animal, then I would most certainly knock her butt out. But she's not out of control. She's a person, and as such, we will conduct any tests in a people place with people tools."

"You have those?" Nev asked, sniffing the tea, the hot steam herbal and pleasant.

"When you live out in the boonies, it's not just the animals that need a hand. In many respects, we're not all that different."

"Maisy's patched the Joneses a few times when we've gotten into trouble that a hospital might report," Jeb admitted, taking the seat beside Nev.

While Jeb's past fascinated her, there was something bugging her. "Why aren't you more shocked by my wings? I mean, I'm sure it's not every day someone comes to see you with bird parts sticking out of their backs."

"I've seen things you can't even imagine." Maisy leaned her elbows on the counter, cradling her mug.

"Some a lot scarier than your wings. Heck, was it two years ago, or three, Jeb, when that Sasquatch from Canada came trekking through and stopped in for your uncle's fiftieth?"

"You saw a Sasquatch?" Nev squeaked.

Jeb laughed. "Ha. So funny, Maisy. Not Larry's fault he was born big and hairy. Everybody knows there's no such thing as a Bigfoot, or a werewolf for that matter."

Maisy frowned. "Haven't you told her—"

"That my family knows some really interesting folks?" Jeb interrupted. "Nope. Didn't want to scare Nev off."

"Fucking hell, Jeb—"

Again, Jeb jumped in. "Language, Maisy. Wouldn't want to offend Angel, here."

Nev gaped. Then laughed. "I'm not offended by the f-word."

"What about ASS?" Maisy asked with a sharp look at Jeb.

He gave Nev's a light tap. "Only one ass worth noticing for me."

The compliment brought heat to Nev's cheeks even as their conversation confused. "My butt is the one thing that hasn't changed."

The mention drew Maisy's gaze. "Can you tell me the differences you've noticed since the experiments started?" The doctor reached over and grabbed a notepad and pen, ready to take notes.

Nev chewed her lower lip. "Should you be writing this down? What if someone finds it?"

"This will help me organize my thoughts and give you a better diagnosis. Once we're done, and you don't need me, you can watch me burn it."

Cloak and dagger stuff. Who would have thought, a

girl emerging from a broken home with a drunk father, a vagrant flitting from place to place, would become involved in such intrigue?

Nev sighed. "Obviously my wings are the most noticeable change."

"Have they always been that size? What about the color of your feathers?"

"They are much bigger. Fuller, too. When I first got them, they were stiff to move, awkward."

Maisy held the plastic tip of the pen against her chin. "Would you say they were like an atrophied muscle? Something that hadn't been used in a while and got stronger the more you flexed them?"

For a second Nev frowned. The description was probably the most apt one as to what she'd experienced. "Yeah. I guess. As for the color, it did change. At first my feathers were fluffy and light gray, but those fell out and I got this set." She fluttered them without even thinking of it, the sun streaming through the windows highlighting the deep gray hue with hints of mauve.

"Have you molted since getting them?"

"Molted?" The word squeaked from her. "I'm not a bird."

"But your wings are avian in nature. Hence, it stands to reason they would have some characteristics in common. Molting is a natural occurrence."

"Not a bird," Nev stubbornly repeated, hunching.

"Not even close," Jeb announced. He leaned closer. "More like a sexy angel."

The heat of his words caused a tremble within, and she found herself blushing again. To regain her composure, she began reciting other changes in her body. "My eyes changed color. Used to be brown, now they're purple. And they glow."

"What causes the glowing?"

"Radioactivity?" was her smart-ass reply. At Jeb's snicker and Maisy's pursed lips, she giggled. "I don't know why they light up. Usually happens when I'm upset." Or if she missed the potty in the dark and hit her foot. Then they lit up as if to mock her poor aim.

"Triggered by an emotional response," mumbled Maisy as she scribbled. "Anything else?"

"I'm stronger."

"What about healing?"

"I heal."

Maisy looked up from her notepad. "Faster than usual? Slower? The same?"

It took Nev moment to reply. "Faster, I guess. Never really paid attention." Or had a chance to really test it. But, then again, what of the times she grabbed those electrified bars? The times her skin sizzled and blistered? By the next day, the marks were gone. She just assumed the burns weren't as bad as she'd thought.

"Diet?"

"No thanks. Love to eat."

"Any restrictions? Urges you didn't have before?"

She shook her head. "If it's on my plate, I'll eat it."

"Menstrual cycle?"

Words to have her blushing again. She couldn't peek at Jeb. Nor could she reply.

"Just nod your head if it's still regular and normal."

Nev bobbed her head and stared at the counter.

"Have you laid any eggs?"

A glare answered that one.

A few more questions about sleep and other mundane

health matters wrapped up the interview. Then Maisy wanted to examine her.

"Mind checking on my menagerie in the barn?" Maisy asked Jeb. To Nev, she said, "I'm sure you'd rather a little privacy for the next part."

Privacy would be nice, yes, but the idea of not having the man she'd come to see as her rock by her side? Part of her panic must have shown because Jeb tilted her chin, catching her gaze. "You'll be fine, Angel. I won't be far."

She nodded and tried to sound brash. "I don't need you holding my hand while she pokes me." Except, as Maisy began to palpate her body and take her vitals, Nev kind of wished he were.

It didn't take long, nor did it hurt. As a matter of fact, it was the easiest exam she'd ever had, and she couldn't help saying something when Maisy declared, "Done," and began peeling off her gloves.

"That's it?"

"Yes."

"No needles?" No intrusive probing of her orifices?

"I will need to draw some blood, and maybe have you pee in a cup, but that can wait if you're tired."

"I don't want to wait." If this woman, with her calm manner, had any ideas on how to help, then Nev was open to them.

She still didn't actually believe Maisy could do anything, but she had nothing to lose from trying.

Jeb returned as Maisy was removing the needle with its vial full of blood.

"Hey, Angel. She making you into a pincushion? Want me to beat her up?" His eyes twinkled as he offered.

Maisy snorted. "As if you would lay a hand on a woman."

"I'd do anything to protect, Angel." He said to Maisy but he winked at Nev, which made her glow on the inside. To Maisy, he remarked. "So, what's the verdict? You got something in that apothecary of yours to help her?"

Maisy's shoulders rolled. "Maybe, but I don't want to rush into anything. I'm going to check some of my recipe books first before throwing stuff at her."

"Recipe books?" Nev queried.

"Handed down by my mother, and her mother before her and so on. Folk remedies you won't find online or in stores."

"And you think you have a remedy for mad scientist experiments?"

"Those with visions of mixing human and animal have existed a long time. This isn't the first time this has been attempted."

The claim caused Nev to blink.

Before she could think of an appropriate response, Jeb stepped in. "Your zoo in the barn is taken care of."

"Thanks. Usually, I have a couple who handle it, but they're on vacation for the next week."

"If you need a hand, you know you can call us."

For some reason this caused Maisy's back to stiffen. "I am fine. I don't need a Jones to come to my rescue."

"You know he didn't have a choice, right?"

"He had choices. Now he gets to live with them."

The cryptic back and forth fascinated, but not enough to stop a yawn.

"Poor thing is exhausted. Let's get some food into you, then bed."

A hearty stew hit the spot, and next thing Nev knew, she'd been bustled into a shower—the steaming hot water ecstasy—and then given a clean outfit, the top modified by

Maisy, who shot a side eye at Jeb, mumbling, "Men. They don't care if they wear the same thing for days in a row."

It was nice to have something fresh and soft to wear. Although it lacked the masculine scent she'd come to enjoy.

The spare bedroom was for Nev alone. It sported the same bright color scheme as the living room, with the walls a vivid orange, the tile on the floor some flowery pattern. The wall art was pictures, mostly outdoor shots blown up and framed. But she cared less about the art than the fact she'd get to sleep in a bed behind a closed door. Privacy and comfort all in one, and yet, she couldn't sleep. She tossed and turned, rolling from her belly to her side, the edge of the bed high enough from the floor that her wings could hang over. Despite the softness of the mattress, she couldn't get comfortable.

Unable to handle it, she rose and opened the door, which led to the main living space. Jeb immediately rose from the couch. "What's wrong?"

For a moment, she couldn't speak. Despite the darkness coating the room, she could see. Enough to realize he wore only his pants, hanging low on his hips. No shirt. Nothing to hide the delineated musculature of his upper body. The perfection of it.

She swallowed. "I, uh, can't sleep."

"Are you stressing?" He started toward her, and she held her ground, letting him get close enough that the heat of his body touched her chilled skin.

"I don't know what's wrong." Except she did know. *I don't want to be alone.* She just couldn't say it aloud.

Somehow, though, he knew. He reached out, his hands palming her waist, drawing her near. "You're not alone, Angel. I'm here."

"For now. You can't babysit me forever." He'd already left her once to do…something. It would happen again, and there was nothing she could do about it.

Loneliness would be her new reality.

"It's not babysitting." He nestled her into the scorching heat of his chest. Her cheek rested on his flesh, and she could feel the steady thump of his heart. "I like being with you."

"You barely know me," she murmured against his chest.

"Funny, because since the moment I met you it felt like I'd known you forever."

A bold statement, and yet one she could understand. They'd met such a short time ago; however, a bond existed between them. She felt a closeness with Jeb, a rightness she couldn't explain that was more than lust. Although desire played a strong part.

She wanted this man.

Wanted to touch him. Kiss him.

What did it say about her that amidst all her problems she wanted to have sex?

It says I'm alive. That I don't know what tomorrow will bring.

"Jeb." She said his name softly, unsure how to ask. How did one say, make me come?

Except he knew. Or he felt the same thing, too.

He lifted her chin and kissed her.

Kissed her long and hard.

Devoured her mouth as his hands roamed her body, touching her and reminding her that, in spite of all that happened, she was still a woman. A woman with needs.

So when he said, "If we don't stop, I'm going to take you right here," she didn't push away.

Rather, she grabbed him by the hand and led him into the bedroom.

She let go of his hand to stand in front of him and stripped her clothes.

Wondering if she made the right choice when he stood staring and didn't say a word.

✻ 14 ✻

Tongue-tied, it took him a moment to say anything after she stripped. Awe didn't cover it.

He'd seen women naked. Hello, he wasn't a virgin, but there was something about the way Nev showed her trust, how she laid herself literally bare before him, that hit him.

He sighed. "You are so damned beautiful."

"I am?" She sounded unsure.

Which was wrong. He needed to show her, show her how she made him feel. He needed to make her feel as insane as he did whenever she was around.

"Come here," he demanded, and yet he was the one to move, to palm her bare waist, his fingers digging into silken skin. He pressed his mouth to hers, inhaling her scent—something fruity from the shampoo meshed with the essence of her.

She moaned against his mouth as they kissed. Her hands tentatively touching him at first, then growing bolder as his mouth devoured hers hungrily. His tongue slid against hers, a sensuous glide that he savored. The brazen temptress replied by sucking on it. Drawing a groan from him.

Their bodies touched, the bare skin of his chest rubbing against hers, the tips of her nipples igniting his arousal. The heat of her skin scorched.

Her hands clutched at his hair, anchoring his head for the kiss, as if he'd dare to move away.

Never.

She clung to him, and he explored her, stroking over the skin of her waist and hips, learning her shape, dipping behind to cup her cheeks.

He dragged his mouth across her jawline to the lobe of her ear, remembering how much she enjoyed it before. He licked and nibbled, gauging her enjoyment by how much she relaxed, her head dropping back, a silent permission for more. As he sucked her tender flesh, his hands cupped the curve of her buttocks, kneading the firm flesh, squeezing. Drawing her pelvis against the hardness straining in his pants.

She shivered, and he knew it wasn't from the cold. They were both too hot for that. She shook with desire.

Soon it would have her crying his name.

He slid a hand between them to cup her mound. She moaned, and her hips thrust, demanding more.

Air kissed his arse as she tugged down his pants, freeing his hard length that she might cup it. He sucked in a breath.

He jerked in her grip as she began to slide her hand up his shaft then back again. It felt so damned good he almost forgot himself.

But the heat of her pulsed against the hand still cupping her. He parted the folds of her sex, the dampness lube for his fingertip.

She uttered a cry as he stroked. He meshed his mouth to hers and caught the next keening sound, the flick of his fingers making her hips jerk.

He thought she would come against his hand, but she suddenly pulled away.

Then shoved him.

He hit the edge of the bed and fell on it. Nev pounced atop him a second later. She straddled him, legs on either side of his hips, hands braced against the mattress. She kissed him again as the head of his cock nudged at her sex.

Slid between her damp lips.

Pushed into her.

Only she teased, sitting just above him, enough he could feel the wet heat.

He grabbed her around the waist and murmured her name. "Nev. Angel. Look at me."

Her eyes blazed. Glowing with passion.

Need...

She lowered herself onto him, her thighs parting wide that he might push into her. His cock stretched the walls of her sex, and she gripped him tight.

Their locked gaze was interrupted by their dual need for a kiss. Their lips meshed as he thrust into her. Pumped into the silken heat of her body.

As he drove deep into her, her nails dug into his chest, the painful bite making him gasp—in pleasure.

She undulated atop him, grinding and swirling her body, her breath hitching with exertion, her skin hot and dewy against his.

Arousal held him tight, and her sex held him even tighter. They were both racing for a peak. Bodies moving in time. Rotating and thrusting.

Her cries turned into ragged gasps. Then she came,

pulsing waves of heat and pleasure. And while it wasn't a scream, she did say his name, "Jeb," and her wings unfurled. A beautiful angel flushed and climaxing.

He came with her. Shooting hotly into her. Marking her with his seed.

Claiming her even if she didn't know it yet.

I know the future scares you, Angel. But I promise we'll face it together.

Waking just as night lightened into dawn, Jeb spent a moment staring at the woman lying beside him in bed.

Her expression appeared peaceful in sleep, the lines of worry smoothed, her lashes a dark band touching the tops of her cheeks. Her hair, soft and fine to the touch, was spread across her pillow. She clung to the blanket, holding it close to her chin, keeping her front warm, but he worried about her backside. Nev slept curled on her side, body scooched to the very edge of the mattress allowing her wings space to hang.

She'd not let him touch her wings last night. Even if every other part of her was his to explore. And explore he had, delighting in her soft skin, her passionate cries.

Yet for all her enjoyment, she held back a part of herself. She didn't fully trust. Didn't believe him when he said she was beautiful.

Her insistence that her wings were ugly was something he'd have to work on. He'd have to find the right words to explain just how glorious he found her feathery appendages. How lucky he felt when she rode him and, in her moment of climax, how the wide flexing sweep truly made her into an angel.

His angel. One who needed her sleep.

Rather than waking Nev, Jeb slipped out of bed, found

his pants and shirt, and tugged them on quietly before he exited the room.

Out in the main living space, the dawn light shone even brighter, the curtains at the wide windows pulled open to let it stream in. He spotted Maisy in the kitchen, bustling around, flipping pancakes on a griddle. Spotting him, she grabbed a mug hanging from a hook and poured him a coffee. She slid it onto the counter as he took as seat on a stool.

"Morning," he said.

"A good one, I'd wager, given whose room you came out of." She arched a brow.

Heat rose in his cheeks. "Erm, yeah. Uh."

She laughed. "Your expression is priceless. I'm not judging. I'm happy for you. Both of you."

"I'm happy, too. I think she's the one." The woman to finally make this 'roo settle down.

Flip. A pancake went from raw dough to golden brown. "Why do you sound so glum about it?"

"Because she has no idea what I am."

"Which was your first mistake. And a surprise. How the hell does she not know? Scent alone—"

He interrupted. "Don't forget, we grew up with the knowledge of what we are. We're taught how to recognize scent. She wasn't. To her, we probably just all smell funny."

"So tell her."

He grimaced. "Tell her, she says. Exactly how do I explain that I am not just a man but a kangaroo, too? That the world she thought she knew is a lie? That shapeshifters exist."

Maisy held the flipper in the air and wagged it at Jeb. "Not a lie, just bigger than she knew. Did it ever occur to you that maybe telling her about cryptids would help her accept what was done to her?"

"Except she's not a cryptid. She's human. Was human," he corrected. "Now she's an experiment. Something that has to be hidden from not only humankind but even our own people. You know what they'll do to her."

"You don't know for sure they'd lock her away."

"Don't I?" He arched a brow. "If we can't hide her wings, then those in authority won't see another choice. If FUC catches her, they'll put her in another prison. Sure, it will be a nicer one—they're not complete bastards—but she won't be free."

"What can you do then?"

He shrugged. "I don't know." An admission he hated to make, especially since he'd fallen in love with her and wanted to take her somewhere far away where no one would ever find her and try to hurt her.

Words he wished he'd said to her because, when he returned to the bedroom to announce breakfast was ready, he found the bed empty, the window open. Nev had flown the coop.

❧ 15 ❧

NEV KNEW what they said about eavesdropping. You never heard anything good, and yet, not long after Jeb slipped from bed, she couldn't help herself. Especially once she heard the murmur of voices. She missed part of the conversation, but she heard enough to make her sad. Heard him say she was human. But the most important thing she heard?

I can't be free. Deny it all he wanted to her face, he spoke the truth to Maisy.

It hurt to realize the night of passion was but a momentary blip. Yes, he was attracted to her. And her to him. The reality remained. She was a freak, and if she stuck around, someone would put her in a cage.

It seemed best if she left. Now. Before she dragged Jeb down with her. She'd seen enough conspiracy movies to know that anyone associated with her might end up locked up, too—or worse.

She took only long enough to throw on some clothes, ignoring the tingling of her body that still recalled—and craved—his touch. Since she couldn't leave via the door, she heaved open the window, wincing at the creak. But the conversation outside the room continued.

She exited the window, silently cursing as her wings got caught on the edges. A bit of wiggling and she got out, but faced a new dilemma. Where to go?

Did it matter?

Anywhere. Away. She began marching, her pace quick.

Not quick enough to escape Jeb, who caught up and marched beside her.

"Going somewhere, Angel?"

She wouldn't look at him. Wouldn't let herself be swayed by his good looks. "Thanks for your help, but it's time I took off and did things on my own."

"Where are you going to go?"

"I don't know."

"Where you going to get money? Food? Clothes? Where will you shelter?"

With every question, her lips stretched until they were a thin line. "I don't know," she finally screeched. "But I have to do something."

"Come back to the house with me."

"Why?" she said, whirling to face him.

"Maisy went through her books—"

"I don't give a damn about her books. Don't you get it? I'm a freak. Drinking some potion, doing some witchy dance, all that old wives' tale mumbo-jumbo won't change the fact I have wings!"

"I understand."

"No, you don't. Look at you." She waved a hand in his direction. "Perfectly normal. You can go anywhere you like. No one will say shit to you. No one will try and lock you up."

"I know a place—"

"To hide me?" She laughed, the sound discordant and bitter. "For how long? Eventually someone will see me. Or videotape the sideshow freak with wings."

"Angel—" He probably meant to say more except there was a blaring of horns. They'd not actually made it far from the house, which meant, when they turned around, they could see the two vehicles that slammed to a halt by the house, dust momentarily covering them.

From one bounced that woman from before—the blonde one—except this time she'd brought a man with her. A big man who wore a sling on his chest for the baby he pulled out of the backseat. While he did that, the blonde marched over to the other vehicle and rapped on the window.

"What the hell is Miranda doing here?" Jeb muttered. "This won't be good."

"You told her I'd be here?"

"Nope. Only people who knew were my brothers. And before you say it, they wouldn't have told."

"So how did they find us?" she asked, arms crossed over her chest.

"I don't know, but I aim to find out. Come on."

"Are you insane? They'll see my wings."

"They already know about them."

"What?"

He didn't reply. His fingers laced through hers, tugging her back toward Maisy's home and driveway.

As they neared, they could hear raised voices. Miranda harangued a man in the second vehicle while the big dude with the baby hung back.

"Who's the guy with the baby?" she asked.

"Miranda's hubby. And that's their joey."

"They brought their baby boy to capture me?" she asked, utterly confused.

"Girl. Name of Kelly, if I recall correctly."

"So they brought their baby girl? Doesn't make it any better," she snapped.

"Means they didn't expect any trouble. Chase is protective of the little mite."

"Who's the other guy?"

The fellow had stepped out of the vehicle finally. Tall, thin, the hair atop his balding pate but a few stubborn strands. He wore a suit, gray slacks and blazer over a white collared shirt, even a tie. He stared down his nose at Miranda, who shook her finger at him.

They got close enough to catch the words.

"...don't appreciate going behind my back. We were handling this."

"The only thing fuck should handle is four-legged furry things. Leave ass business alone."

The foul language surprised Nev. Especially given the fellow looked rather uptight. Her head spun trying to keep up.

"We don't know for sure it's ass business."

"She has wings." Making it pretty clear why he was here. His hand swept in Nev's direction for emphasis. Spotted.

"Is it too late to run?" she whispered.

"Don't worry, Angel. Despite how it looks, these people won't hurt you." Jeb tried to reassure, but Nev had a bad feeling.

Miranda shook her head, and her blonde hair bounced. "Just because she's got wings doesn't automatically make her one of yours."

"Council says she is," the guy in the suit said smugly.

"You told the council about her?" screeched Miranda.

"Who's the council?" Nev asked Jeb, whose fingers had tightened around hers.

"The people who govern ass, fuck, and everyone else."

"There are people governing that?" she said, her eyes wide open.

"No. Not how you think. Shit." He turned to her. "Listen, there's things I haven't told you. Things I had to keep secret."

She stared at him, spotting the worry in his gaze. "Did you tell them I was here?"

"No. Of course not. But despite my efforts, they know about you. Apparently, they've found a way to track you."

"I'm so confused."

"I promise to explain everything. Just give me a chance."

"No more chances for you. Step away from the woman." The man in the suit approached, an annoyed-looking Miranda at his heels.

"You can't just barge in on an active investigation," Miranda harangued.

"Quiet, rabbit, or I'll have you brought up on charges of obstruction, meddling—"

"Watch your tone, Mr. Boviary," the baby daddy rumbled. "That's my honey you're threatening."

While the big man didn't do anything, Boviary blanched. "Tell your wife this is ass business."

"But fuck—"

"Has no jurisdiction."

Wide-eyed, Nev watched the exchange and finally blurted, "My ass belongs to me. You ain't taking it and whoring it."

Boviary blinked at her. "What are you talking about, woman?"

"My name is Nevaeh."

"And I am Francois Boviary, ass agent."

Jeb muttered, "Ass stands for Avian Soaring Security. Think of them as law enforcement and governing body for all aerial cryptids."

"What's a cryptid?" Nev asked.

"People who are not pure human."

"Like me," she said.

"Like all of us," Boviary announced. "Of course, some of us are more evolved than others." His words only confused the issue.

"He just insulted me, Chase," Miranda growled as her husband held her back.

"I don't understand," Nev stated. "What's he saying? What's going on?"

"Does the woman not know?" Boviary asked with some surprise.

"No," Jeb replied.

"What don't I know?" Nev asked, unable to stop herself from sounding cross.

"Oh, for carrot's sake. Someone needs to explain to the girl. Honey"—Miranda faced her—"we're shapeshifters."

"Hunh?" Because the claim made no sense.

Boviary sighed. "Who will demonstrate?"

"Demonstrate what?" Nev asked, understanding something was happening but unable to figure it out.

For some reason, Miranda peeled off her shirt then her pants. Nev felt her rage growing as the woman denuded herself in front of Jeb. Felt her fingers extend into claws. Knew her eyes must be glowing.

Then assumed she was losing her mind because, next

thing she knew, Miranda wasn't there anymore. But a giant bunny with great big fangs was!

"She's— She's—" Nev couldn't quite spit it out.

"She's a shapeshifter. And an agent for fuck which stands for Furry United Coalition," Jeb explained.

"And he's…" Nev pointed to Boviary.

"A bird."

"Show me," she said to the prim and proper man. Because, in spite of the bunny, she still didn't quite believe.

Stripping and folding his clothes first, Boviary turned into a man-sized bird, all long legs, orange beak, and spotted plumage.

She blinked. "Who else is an animal here?"

Maisy, who'd been standing silently behind them this entire time said, "I'm a kitty."

Again, Nev didn't believe it until she saw it. A big black panther with vivid yellow eyes. Then there was the bear, who cradled the baby in his arms. A menagerie of animals. She looked at Jeb. Finally grasping the truth but wanting to see it with her own eyes.

"Show me."

"I wanted to tell you," he said, apology in his gaze.

"Show. Me."

And he did. His body melted and reshaped into a kangaroo of all things.

The man she'd slept with. The man she'd trusted.

A liar.

No wonder he'd never had a problem with her wings.

"You're a freak, too," she murmured, part shock, part wonderment. They all were.

"Not freaks. We are cryptids. Or, if you prefer the more modern term, shapeshifters." Boviary had turned back into himself—his human self. "And you are one of us.

We've been trying to find you since the institute burned down."

"You knew about me?"

"Only recently. FUC was holding back information. It was only by chance that we learned of your existence. We immediately requested you be turned over."

"So you could lock me up," she hotly retorted.

Boviary didn't feign his surprise. "Why would we do that?"

"Because I'm a freak." She fluttered her wings.

"You are one of us."

"You mean to say you're okay with me running around with these puppies?" Again, she fluttered them.

"For safety reasons, we obviously can't allow you to be seen by humans. However, we do have a place for you to go where you will be safe. Free. Where no one will think it odd you have wings. With others of your kind. The aerie can provide you a home. Something these people have neglected to tell you." The man with the long, stork-like legs and beakish nose glared at the assembled motley group, undaunted by his nudity.

Meanwhile Nev wanted to sink into the ground. Maybe scream a little. Definitely wished for some towels or blankets to cover up all the folk when they returned to their less hairy selves. Except for Jeb. Jeb looked mighty fine naked.

For a liar.

"You're a kangaroo," she exclaimed, jabbing her finger at him.

"Yeah."

"And you didn't tell me."

He shifted, looking uncomfortable. "Wasn't sure how."

"Rules prevented him from saying anything," Maisy interjected, earning a dark look from Nev.

"You lied, too. And while I don't know the rest of you"—she shot a glare all around—"I'll bet you all would have lied."

"Our existence is not something to be shared with mere humans," announced Boviary.

"But I'm not human, anymore," Nev shouted, her wings lifting and spreading in agitation. "And you let me think I was an aberration."

"I wanted to tell you—" Jeb exclaimed.

"But you didn't. You didn't tell me that there were others like me. That I had a place to go."

"The aerie is a tightly guarded secret. I wasn't sure they'd take you."

"Did you ask?" she inquired, a tad too sweetly. "Did you call up anyone and say hey, got myself a bird lady. You guys got room for her?" Before he could reply, she yelled, "No, you didn't. How could you?" Left unsaid were the words I trusted you.

Funny how his betrayal hurt worse than anything else that hurt her before.

❦ 16 ❦

ANGEL'S VOICE BROKE, and something inside Jeb broke with her.

He held out pleading hands. "I'm sorry. Angel—"

"Don't you Angel me. You should have told me."

"I was going to."

"When? Before we had sex? Oh, that's right. We already did that. So when, Jeb? When would you have told me I had a place to go? People who would accept me for who I am? A place where I didn't have to hide?"

The words cut through him because, the truth was, he had been afraid. Afraid that if she knew there might be somewhere for her to go that she would leave.

Leave me.

And now, the nightmare was coming true. She was striding toward Boviary. "Take me to this aerie place. I'm tired of running and hiding."

"At once." Boviary shot him a look of triumph as he quickly dressed.

Jeb wasn't about to let her go though, not without saying something.

He followed her to the van, catching her before she entered.

"Angel, please. Just listen. I'm sorry. I should have said something. But I was afraid for you. I didn't want anyone taking you from me."

"So this was about you?" She shot him a look. "What about me? About my needs?"

"I would have—"

"What? Found a bigger treehouse to stash me in? Paid me visits when you felt like it? Goodbye, Jebediah."

She climbed into the van and slammed the door.

He could only stare at the mirrored glass and whisper, "But I love you."

Loving Angel didn't stop the van from leaving.

Maisy put a hand on his shoulder. "I'm sorry."

Not as sorry as he was. He couldn't help sounding dejected when he said, "I just wanted to keep her safe."

"I know. Once she stops being angry, I'm sure she'll see it, too."

"And then what?" he asked. "Do you really think she'll want to leave a place where she doesn't have to hide?" Why would she leave to be with him?

"The aerie is a nice place I'm sure, but there's one thing it's missing," Maisy remarked. "You."

Yeah, which was probably something Nev would appreciate, given the way he'd stalled on telling her the truth.

"If it's any consolation, I was trying to get here before him," Miranda noted, having gotten dressed. She now balanced the baby girl on her hip. "Somehow he got here ahead of me."

"I appreciate it. Although you could have called."

"Tried. No reception."

Maisy shrugged. "The disadvantages of living in the boonies. Erratic signal."

A warning would have only delayed the inevitable. "Guess I should head back home." Deal with the ribbing from his brothers that he'd lost his angel. The backlash from FUC because ASS was sure to complain.

The ride home in his truck—after he dressed in some spare clothes he kept under the seat—was spent dejected.

Until his 'roo finally had enough and jumped into his skin long enough to bounce his face off the steering wheel. Jolted, he slammed the truck to a stop and glared at himself in the rearview mirror.

"What the fuck was that for?" he snapped. Usually he and his inner beast were in perfect harmony. But on rare occasions when they didn't see eye-to-eye, his other half could make himself a pest.

Idiot. Shouldn't have let her go.

I didn't have a choice.

Fight.

Fight who? ASS? That wouldn't have gone over well.

His 'roo tried to ram his face off the steering wheel again, but he managed to keep a grip. "Stop it."

No. You should have fought for her. Told her she's our mate. Told her—

"I love her. Oh, fuck me, I never said it, did I?" Shown it, yes. Felt it. Yes. Even known it, but when had he ever said anything to her? All this time she assumed he'd helped her because...he was a nice guy helping a lady in distress. He never explained there was something more to it.

Love at first sight.

Instinct.

Fate.

"Bloody hell, you're right."

Smugness was his reply.

"I need to go after her. Find her. Tell her I love her. Wings and all. Beg her forgiveness and see if she'll have me as her mate."

Finally, his 'roo hopped in approval. He thrust the truck into gear and sped for home, planning what he'd have to do. Mammals weren't welcome in the aerie unless they got special dispensation. He might have to pull some strings. Or at the very least find some way of communicating with someone on the inside.

He needed to talk to Nev.

Excited about the prospect of making things right, he never noticed the other vehicle that came out of nowhere and slammed into his truck.

17

N<small>EV LEFT</small>, heart dragging more than her feet.

A part of her screamed she should stay and talk to Jeb. She could kind of see how hard it would be to admit what he was.

But, at the same time, she was so mad at him. He'd left her thinking she was an aberration. A monster even.

Didn't once tell her she wasn't alone.

For that she hated him. Which was why she'd left.

Boviary had come prepared. The vehicle he drove was some kind of modified Econoline van. The cargo space, which ran the entire length behind the driver's seat, had a bench running down the middle raised high enough she could perch on it without her wings getting in the way.

The bench was hard, but it helped her to ignore Jeb, standing with a forlorn expression outside the window. Oh, that face. That sad, sad face.

She almost lost her resolve. Almost jumped out of that van to accept his apology. Then she remembered how that story ended. She'd grown up with it.

Her dad used to do that. Look all pitiful and asking for

forgiveness. Once he sobered up, that was. Daddy usually meant it, too, until the next time he got wasted.

Words were fickle.

People couldn't be trusted. Especially liars.

The van lurched into motion, and she kept staring straight ahead, ignoring the man she left behind. The ache in her heart was trepidation at what lay ahead and not because of whom she left behind.

Only once they'd put a few miles behind them did she grasp what she'd done.

Left probable safety with an absolute stranger.

Who also had wings.

A man she knew nothing about.

She stared at the back of Boviary's head.

What have I done?

"Where are we going?" she asked, breaking the silence.

"To the aerie."

Which didn't mean diddly-squat to her. "What is the aerie?"

He never took his eyes from the road as he replied. "It's where all those with wings belong. A secret place, nestled in the heart of New Zealand within a dormant volcano that has long been home to one of the first sentient flocks."

The word flock threw her but not as much as— "By sentient, you mean…"

"People who learned how to call forth their avian side. Who have evolved to the next level."

"Do you think that's what happened to me? Did the Bunyip Institute shove my body into the next stage of human evolution?"

"I am not a scientist who can reply to that."

Perhaps not, but imagining herself as having transcended to a new level was a much better thought than the one that those scientists had spliced her with mutated DNA.

"It would make sense though. If this is the next stage of human evolution—"

"Not the next one for everyone. Only some people have that kernel of possibility in them. Some more than others. Whereas some end up with a hairier outcome."

"You're talking about that bunny and bear and Jeb, aren't you?"

"The mammalian faction. A populous group given they do internal gestation. Grunting out their young in barbaric fashion."

She blinked. "How else would they give birth?"

"The truly evolved use the ovi method."

"Which means?"

"The laying of eggs and the ritual fertilizing them."

"Eggs as in the kind you crack and eat scrambled with milk and cheese?"

Ever realize you'd said the wrong thing as you said it?

Nev bit her lip.

Boviary stared stiffly ahead. "While the cannibalism of the non-sentient ova is allowed within our laws, it should never be used, even in a joking manner, with another of the avian race. It is considered extremely gauche."

"F-bomb bad, eh?"

"Worse."

"Sorry. Just a little freaked out. You keep acting like I'm some kind of bird, and yet, I'm not."

"Your flavor is unique."

"Flavor?" A word that really had her second-guessing her choice to get in the van with this man.

"Your scent. Are you truly that clueless?" Boviary met her gaze in the rearview mirror and tsked. "You were told nothing. Not even the most basic thing, which is scent is our version of a fingerprint. Each one is unique."

"I don't know if that's cool or gross."

"It is what it is. We use smell to identify many things, including what a person is. A true professor of scent can even trace lineage down to a family flock."

"Would they be able to tell me what I am?" Dove? Raven? She couldn't think of many birds with her color of plumage.

"They will know what you are."

Really? Because she wouldn't mind knowing. "The way you talk, there's a lot of you guys."

"Us guys?" He gave the words a note of disdain. "The flock should not be disparaged. Nor should you ever conflate us with those mammals." He curled his disgust around the last syllable.

"But aren't you a mammal right now?"

"An unfortunate disguise. One day, when the phoenix rises from the ashes, we shall shed these skins and soar the skies freely as we are meant to."

"Sounds like you have some kind of Alfred Hitchcock bird manifesto."

"You'll learn. In the aerie you will receive an education on the ways of the flock."

"You're sending me to school?"

"Given your lack of knowledge, yes."

"But I already graduated from high school."

"Human school. You need to learn flock history and biology."

So long as they didn't mind if she snickered the first time she saw a man or woman squatting over an egg to keep it warm.

"By the sounds of it, the flock is pretty large. And the, um, other guys—"

"You can call those who are not human cryptids."

"Er, cryptids seem like they're all over. So how is it I never heard of this before? I mean except for like the movies and stuff."

"Because we guard the secret. We've been guarding it for centuries. Since mankind truly began evolving. We learned early on that acceptance wasn't something we could count on. Humans do so love to persecute and kill that which they fear."

"But you're taking me to this aerie place, so I don't have to worry, right?"

"The aerie itself is hidden. There will be no one to scream about your appearance. Not even the passing satellites can penetrate. It is one of the few places in the world we don't have to hide our true selves."

It sounded too good to be true. "Won't people still look at me weird because I can't hide my wings?"

He shot her a brief glance. "While a partial shift is not common, it does happen. People caught in mid morph, unable to fully turn one way or the other. Happens sometimes with adolescents who don't have full control and with the elderly, especially if dementia sets in."

"You're talking of people born like that. I wasn't. I'm not supposed to be able to shift."

"And yet here you are."

"Because the scientists changed me." The bitter words spilled out.

"Which is why you won't be in trouble for not reporting to the nearest ASS agency."

"How could I be in trouble? I never even knew you existed. Ass is supposed to be something you shake. And who was the idiot who called you guys ASS in the first place?"

It didn't take much to offend Boviary. He stiffened. "While the acronym is only recent, our agency has been around for quite some time. We conduct operations almost daily in the service of the flocks."

"Am I one of those operations?"

"You are."

"How did your agency know about me?" How had he found her? She never did ask.

"When the Bunyip Institute was dismantled, all the recovered hard drives were scoured for information. Most of them were wiped. Still, we did get some trace remains of files."

"Were you able to find out anything about me?"

"Nothing other than what we've discussed or I've seen. No records remained of the institute test subjects. Even the security videos the cameras taped are gone. Still, we did find one important thing: A signal for a tracking beacon."

She blinked. "Excuse me?"

"It is very common for science labs to tag subjects with electronic location chips. In case they get lost."

"Or escape," she muttered. She peered down at herself. "Where is it? If there's a tracking thing in my body, then I want it out."

"I'm afraid that could be difficult. The chips are quite tiny and hard to locate once in the body."

Nev grimaced. "Then how do we stop it from broadcasting?" Because if Boviary found her, then so could someone else.

"You'll see," was his cryptic reply. "I think we're far enough now we can take care of it."

Far enough from what? Or was that who?

Boviary pulled the van over and parked it. He hopped out and opened the doors in the back. "If you could please join me for a moment."

He gestured. She slid down the bench and out into the blazing sun. They were in the middle of nowhere. Literally. Just hard-packed dirt with a few scraggly bushes.

"Now what?" she asked. Was this where he suddenly pulled out a cleaver and announced she was dinner? It might scare her enough to lay an egg.

Boviary reached into the van and pulled out a hard-plastic case. "If you'll follow me away from the van."

Because God forbid he get blood on it. More certain than ever she was going to die, she lagged behind Boviary as he put some distance between them and the vehicle.

She stopped, her nerves pulled taut. "What are you going to do?"

"We are going to disable—" He'd turned to speak to her and frowned. "What are you doing over there? You need to be closer, or this won't work."

"Are you going to kill me?"

Boviary's mouth pinched. "I am not an animal."

His look of disgust pulled her closer until she stood beside him, ready to sprint if he suddenly pulled out a gun or a knife.

Kneeling on the hard ground, Boviary opened the case. He peeled back a cloth revealing a bulbous-looking galactic blaster.

"Did you buy that at Toys 'R' Us?"

"Hardly. This is a supersonic electromagnetic pulse emulsifier."

There was only one thing to ask after that mouthful. "Is it going to turn me into a puddle?"

"No, but it will disable the tracker and scramble any electronics within fifteen yards."

Which explained why they'd moved away from the vehicle.

"Arms out to your side," he instructed. "Don't move. This might hurt a bit." He aimed, and a green light went on as the alien pistol emitted a high-pitched squeal.

Her body didn't react at first, and she almost relaxed. Then the burning pain hit in her thigh.

THE CELL JEB woke in was a barren one. Then again, it could have had all kinds of luxuries—a mattress, carpeting, television, fridge—and it wouldn't have changed the fact he was a prisoner.

What the heck happened? His last recollection was driving back home, moping about how he'd fucked things up with Nev. Then *wham*.

Someone rammed him. But he'd obviously not been seriously injured because he found himself in a cell. Alive.

Standing from the cot, he stretched his limbs, feeling stiff and a little sore. Not unusual given the accident.

"Hallloooo," he called out, still hoping he'd been stuck in here by human authorities. However, his reply came in the form of a gurgle from the cell across from him. A lump rose, the coiled serpent growing, its human arms sticking out from its sides. But that was the only humanity left. The eyes were pure viper, yellow and slitted. A forked tongue flicked as it stared at Jeb.

"Du-u-u-de." He stretched the word. "What happened to you?"

The reply was a hiss.

"Not the talkative type, are you?" he said.

Hiss.

"He can't talk anymore, and I doubt he even understands," another voice croaked from farther up.

Jeb approached the bars but hesitated before touching them, remembering the last cell he'd come in contact with.

"Are the bars electrified?"

"Yup. And the place is wired for sleeping gas, too, if things get rowdy. Gotta keep the animals in line."

"Who are you?" Jeb asked, still straining to see, but the speaker stood just out of sight.

"I am a man who was fooled by a pretty face." As the voice lost its raspy edge, something about it seemed familiar.

"How long you been in that cage?"

"How long since your attack on the institute?"

"You were there?"

A chuckle rumbled. "I was the one in charge of the evacuation. The one who was too slow, apparently."

The meaning of the words made him frown. "Am I speaking to Kole?"

"In the fur."

"But why are you in a cell? I thought you were in charge."

"I am. Was. However, as I said, circumstances intervened and made it impossible for me to remain in control."

"What happened?"

"I failed one time too many, and this is my punishment."

"If you ask me, you deserve more for what you did."

"You might be right, in which case perhaps this is fitting punishment."

Hearing a rustle, Jeb peered best as he could in the direction of the voice. It wasn't a great angle, but enough he could see in the next cell over and across from him. See the fuzzy mammal with a curling mustache and...wings?

"Why the hell would you experiment on yourself?"

"I didn't."

Before Jeb could ask who had, he heard the clacking of heels as someone approached. The perfume scent of a woman coasting ahead on the air currents. Not just any woman.

She came to a stop in front of his cell, red lipstick, red dress.

And still with the wild, auburn hair.

Jeb gaped. "Mum?"

19

THE AERIE WAS as beautiful as Boviary proclaimed. A city chiseled out of the sides of the volcano, terraced to provide platforms, some holding lush gardens. Others paced with stone and set with comfortable seating. Some had nothing but T-shaped perches. Because not everyone liked to sit on their butts.

This was a place for the birds.

Which, in her past life, she would have mocked. Ogled. Probably cracked a few jokes about nests and birdseed.

Before she would have.

Now, the aerie felt like home. It provided peace and relaxation.

In the aerie, no one looked oddly at Nev. Her wings were considered normal. Heck, her wings were the only reason they allowed her in. Her wings meant immediate acceptance, no matter how she'd gotten them.

She would admit, though, that, despite the fact she had feathers, it took a little getting used to seeing giant birds walking around. She quickly learned not to hum the theme to *Sesame Street* around them, ask them if they'd seen Snuffleupagus, or do the chicken dance. Not everyone appreciated her sense of comedy. Many were humorless asses. Real asses, not the Avian Soaring Security kind.

The agents who questioned her wanted to know everything. She ended up telling her story a few times. Underwent some tests with doctors. Even had one of their special sniffers out to figure out what bird of a feather she was.

So far, they had no idea.

While her wings made her belong, her lack of a proper flock to call her own made her an outsider. She appreciated the kindness Boviary and the others showed her, bringing her somewhere where she could be safe and free, but she wanted to escape. Not because she didn't like the aerie, she did. *I miss Jeb.*

Missed him like she'd never missed anything in her life. Which she didn't understand.

In the past, she'd always been able to walk away from stuff. Left folks she met with nary a second thought. She didn't form attachments. Didn't think she was capable of caring for anyone but herself.

Until him.

Jeb left a hole in her life, one that ached for his smile, that yearned for his laugh, that craved his touch.

Maybe she should have listened to him. Forgiven him. Maybe they could have made things work.

He is, after all, a monster like me. No, not a monster. None of these people were. Nor were they freaks. They were cryptids. She liked Pansy's—a night owl assigned as her guide in this new world—explanation best. *Think of us as enhanced versions of humanity. Living in harmony with our animal selves.*

Except Nev's wasn't born but given. Even then Pansy

wouldn't let Nev put herself apart. *You might not have been able to tap your inner self before, but no matter what those scientists and doctors did, you wouldn't have changed at all if the potential wasn't already in you.*

In other words, *I was always a birdbrain.*

And Jeb was a kangaroo. Which, in retrospect, fascinated. Legends only had wolves pulling the whole-body switcheroo. The idea that there was a whole Noah's Ark worth of shapeshifters boggled the mind. She wanted to meet them. See them for herself. Not exactly something that would happen if she stayed in the aerie. Yet what choice did she have? The wings still jutted from her back. That part hadn't changed.

And even if they did agree to let her go, where would she go to? Would Jeb want her back given how rudely they'd parted ways?

The problem also remained, how could they be together if she had to hide?

Entering her room, she didn't need to flick on any lights given the balcony doors spilled sunshine into the space.

They'd given her the equivalent of a loft. High ceilings made of dome rock with wooden poles sticking from it. Round windows set overhead while, on the floor level, there was a huge sliding glass door.

The room had the basics. Full-sized bed with nightstand on either side. Hammock. A table with two chairs and even a loveseat facing a flat screen television. Pansy told Nev if she made the request, they'd even set her up with a game system of her choice.

It was the perfect bachelorette pad, and it was rent free, all because of her wings.

Drifting to the balcony, she gripped the rail as she stood outside, the strong wind gusts, encouraged by hidden fans in the mountainside to create drafts, tugging at her hair.

She watched as birds—people in touch with their feathery selves—coasted along, wings spread, catching the air currents.

Flying free.

No hiding here, just as Boviary had promised.

The dormant volcano provided a natural barrier to the outside world. As to those who might pass overhead? She'd asked it of her guide.

"Can't anyone passing overhead see what's going on?" Nev asked.

"Hologram," Pansy announced as if it were the most normal and natural thing in the world. Whatever the case, it meant being able to fly with the wind in their face and sun on their feathers.

Not that she would know. She'd yet to hit the training stadium where Pansy offered to teach her. Apparently, the expression shoving a baby bird out of the nest to teach it to fly wasn't true. Only rarely did parents resort to that old-school method.

Nowadays—within the volcano itself, in a cavern adapted for their use—fledglings had a huge stadium with a bouncy, padded floor to soften landings if wings should not unfurl or flap hard enough.

Maybe one day she'd give it a try. According to the doctors who examined her since her arrival she was built to fly.

Where would she soar if she had the courage?

Back to—

Ring. Ring. Odd. She didn't have a phone. Yet, the insistent ring continued, forcing her to hunt it down until she found it buried in a basket of fruit someone had dropped off that morning.

Pulling the flip phone from under the grapefruit, she held it in her hand and stared at it. She'd never seen it before. And it obviously wasn't accidentally dropped given how deep she had to dig for it.

As to who called? The phone had taken her too long to find. The missed call from the unknown number teased her.

Was it for me?

Who would be calling? And where did the phone come from?

It rang again, startling her, but she only let it chime twice before answering it with a tentative, "Hello?"

"Yo, is this Nevaeh?"

"Maybe," she said, hedging.

"Sweet. Just the chick I was looking for."

Her brow creased. "Who is this?"

Instead of replying with a name, the man said, "Jeb's in trouble."

At the mention of his name, she straightened, and her blood ran cold. "What happened?"

"Don't have time to explain. If you wanna be part of our brother's rescue mission, get to the observation point on the western lip of the volcano."

"I can't. I'm not allowed to leave." Boviary and the other agents had explained the importance of her not being seen.

"Are you a prisoner?"

"Not exactly."

"We can bust you out if you need help."

Given the people who'd died the last time Jeb and his brothers broke into a place, she hastily replied, "No. No need to bust."

"Good. Then be there in fifteen minutes or we'll be going to save Jeb without you."

Fifteen?

The line went dead before she could reply. If she could have, she would have told the caller no way she could make it in that amount of time. Not walking, anyhow. The western lip was too far. Probably a few miles of hallways and stairs between her apartment and the spot he mentioned.

I'll never make it in time, even if I run. But there was another way. A quicker way.

She looked out the door to her balcony. The western terrace was right across from her. Just a simple two-minute glide and she'd be on the far side and could sprint up a staircase to go higher.

Two minutes of trusting her wings wouldn't get her killed. And for what?

What good could I do? It wasn't as if she could help Jeb. His brothers were trained soldiers, and she was just a girl with wings.

But if Kole and the lady in red had taken him, then she did have a score to settle. And dammit it all, she owed Jeb. Owed him for saving her, more than once. Owed him for giving her freedom.

Owed him a kiss and an apology for flying away out of fear. Leaving him to be with others of her kind didn't make her happy. He made her happy.

And she had—*oh shit*—thirteen minutes to prove it.

No time to think twice.

No time to remember her teacher's lessons on gravity.

She stood on the balcony, took a deep breath, and jumped off.

❦ 20 ❦

SHOCK VIBRATED through Jeb as the woman in red approached. A woman with no apology on her face. A face he could barely remember because she'd abandoned him.

It caused him to prowl the cage, more feline than 'roo, an urge to snarl tugging at his lips. "You did this to me? What the hell is wrong with you?" Jeb snapped.

His mum, because there was no doubt about her identity now that they were face to face, stopped in front of the bars to his cage. He waited to see some sign of remorse, anything rather than her flat expression.

She cocked her head, and her rouged lips pursed. "Is that any way to greet your mother?"

"I'd say it was rather polite given it appears as if you stuck me in this cage." Did the woman, who'd coldly abandoned her family, actually have the brass balls needed to imprison her own son?

"I did." Still with no apology for her actions.

"Why?" A question that covered so many things. *Why imprison me? Why did you leave? Why are you working with*

Kole? Why didn't you love me like a mother is supposed to love her son?

"Given you're a Jones, it seemed safer to put you behind bars."

"Afraid because you did me and my brothers wrong?" he said with a sneer.

A moue of distaste quirked her lips. "Ah, yes, the other hooligans. You know, I should have listened to my own mother when she told me I was marrying beneath me. However, I was young. I let lust and a need to escape my life trick me into settling for the wrong man."

"Wrong man?" He couldn't help an incredulous note. "You had six kids with Da."

"Like I said, lust can make even a woman do foolish things. But after Jaxon was born, I began to realize being a mother wasn't what I was meant for. You should have seen my poor hands." She held out the perfectly manicured fingers. "Callused and cracked from dishes and laundry. I was so tired all the time. You boys…" She shook her head. "Always getting into mischief. Breaking things. Fighting and hollering. I couldn't stand it anymore. Then I met Kole."

"You left Da for that furry fucker?" The very idea she'd chosen that short, pudgy koala over his big, strong father almost had him punching the bars.

"I see you're wondering why." Her lips curled into a sly smile. "Let's just say his ideas aligned better with mine than your father's did."

"You abandoned us. Your flesh and blood."

She made a disparaging noise. "Don't act as if I dumped you on the street. I knew you'd be taken care of. The Joneses are a tight lot. Once a Jones always a Jones."

She rolled her eyes. "Which is why I knew I had to die if I wanted your father to let me go."

The way she stated her perfidy so matter-of-factly boggled the mind.

"You made us think you were dead. You were our mum. Did you not give a shit about us at all?" Jeb could hardly believe this cold woman was the mother he'd put on a pedestal all these years. Granted, his recollections of her were hazy. He was quite young when she left. Still, did she not have any maternal instinct at all?

"Six births and each one a boy. Each more rambunctious than the next. Meanwhile, all I ever wanted was a daughter. Kole helped me with that."

"So it's true. That girl we've seen in the pictures, she's our sister then?"

"Not quite. I wasn't about to go through another pregnancy, thank you very much. But the egg they used was mine, and I did have a hand in designing your sister."

"Designing?" he sputtered. For a moment, he forgot where he was and clasped the bars. Electricity zinged through his fingers and burnt his skin. "Jeezus!" he yelped, yanking them away, leaving some flesh behind. His hands throbbed as blisters immediately formed.

"Way too much of your father in you," she said with a disapproving air.

Which, right then and there, seemed like a good thing to him. Because, in that moment, he didn't want to be related at all to the woman in front of him.

"What do you want with me?"

"You? Nothing really. What need do I have for a common kanga? It's not as if you're rare. Or have a special skill other than fighting." Her lip curled.

"Then why am I in a cage?"

"Because I'm going to use you as a bargaining chip."

He frowned. "Bargain for what?" Because the Joneses, while financially comfortable, didn't have much to offer. They spent quite a bit of their earnings steering clear of courts and trouble—and buying the newest gadgets and toys.

"I'm going to exchange you for the girl. The one you stole."

"Nev?" He blinked at his mother. "What do you want with Nev?"

"Kole mistakenly left her behind when we evacuated the old place. We tracked her to the ranch, but somehow she got away."

"You mean we kicked the arses of your little army, don't you?"

"A temporary victory. And given it's mostly your fault, it's rather appropriate that you're going to help me get her back."

"I am not helping you do shit." As if he'd help his mother capture Nev. At least she was safe in the aerie. Those birdbrains might be flighty, but they wouldn't hand her over.

"You may not be willing to help, but your brothers are. I told them if they wanted you back alive to bring me the girl. They are on their way as we speak."

"Like hell they are." Surely his brothers wouldn't cave to blackmail.

"Apparently they're fonder of you than a genetic experiment."

"You can't do this. I won't let you do this."

"And how will you stop me, *son*?" The mockery on the word made him see red.

Jeb began to pummel at the bars, his rage bubbling

over. But his mum walked away. Heels clacking. Not giving a damn.

Again.

"No." Like hell. He punched the bars some more, bruising his fists. He changed into his 'roo; however, kicking did nothing but singe the soles of his feet, the electricity a never-ending supply.

No escape. No mercy.

How was he supposed to save his angel?

MAKING it across the volcano to the other side ended up not being scary at all. Rather, elation filled Nev as the warm breezes lifted her wings and helped her soar to her target. Banking past her initial destination, all the way to the top of the volcano.

Turned out it wasn't that hard. Flying required flapping to gain altitude and extending her feathery appendages to then coast on currents. She now better understood the expression "light as a feather."

It was landing that proved a tad more difficult. But Nev did it, her feet skidding across the rocky lip of the volcano, stumbling and cursing until she wobbled to a stop.

Then she had to wait and wonder how she'd get picked up. Jeb's brother hadn't exactly given her clear instructions.

Nev watched the sky, a clear blue sky, the sun bright, only the specs of birds—real ones or shifter kind—dotting the horizon.

She shielded her gaze and thus didn't see anyone

approach, which meant, when a gruff voice said, "Are you Nevaeh?" she screamed.

Whirling, she saw a square-faced man, dressed in black combat gear, who would have seemed a lot scarier if he didn't look so much like Jeb.

"I'm Nev. And you are?"

"Jeremy. Jeb's big brother." He held out his hand and shook hers.

"What's wrong with Jeb?"

"I'll explain once we're in the air. Ready to go?"

"Go where?" And how? The man didn't have wings.

"Down. I'll need you to hold on please." He turned around and indicated his broad back.

It was then she noticed the rope tethered at his waist.

She wanted to argue. Rappel down a volcano, was he nuts? But she kept remembering the phone call. Jeb needed her help.

So, she wrapped her arms around Jeremy's neck and her legs around his waist then closed her eyes as he jumped over the side of the mountain.

The jolt wasn't as hard as expected as he hit the side of the volcano with his feet.

Being tucked so close to him she heard the faint electronic voice from the piece nestled in his ear.

"The patrols have resumed. I couldn't hold them off any longer."

"Shit," Jeremy muttered. "Hold on tight. We're gonna have to move faster."

"Why?" she asked.

"Because the birdies don't like people getting close to their nest."

She might have said more, except Jeremy began leaping faster, swinging his body out from the rock, dropping, then hitting the side again before the next bounce.

They were about halfway down the mountain when she heard the shouts. Peering overhead, she saw tiny smudges, faces peeking down at them. But those worried her less than the fact that the next jump had Jeremy cursing as the line holding them lurched.

They spun in midair before hitting the rock, part of the impact catching her wing. She grunted in pain as Jeremy exhorted, "Hang on. This is gonna get tricky."

She wondered what he meant, only to stare wide-eyed as he cut the rope tethering them. They clung to the rock face.

Not a moment too soon. The shorn end disappeared from sight as those above hauled it upward.

A hammering of a spike in the wall tethered their new anchor spot, and she barely had a moment to gulp air when they were flying again, bouncing down. But she must have loosened her grip, or her arms were tired. Whatever the reason, when Jeremy stumbled and jostled them against the rock face, she slipped.

Fell right off his back, her mouth open in a silent cry of surprise.

It might have ended badly for her had Jeb's brother not shouted, "Fucking fly!"

The words galvanized her. She rolled in the air to her stomach and spread her wings. Just in time, too. Catching a current, she skimmed the tops of the trees she'd almost crashed into.

I'm flying.

Elation filled her, and laughter bubbled from her lips. Only to fizzle as she heard a crack of gunfire. *Is someone shooting at me?*

Banking, she flapped her wings and managed to hover for a glance behind at the volcano. It wasn't her being shot at but Jeremy, who was a black speck on the mountain, hopping left and right, working his way down. Meanwhile, above him…

With a determined expression, she flapped and flapped, heading for Jeremy, hoping she was right and that they wouldn't dare shoot at one of their own.

Sure enough, as soon as she got close, there were shouts and the gunfire stopped.

She heard Pansy yelling, "Nev, come back."

"I can't. Jeb needs me."

"You belong here," Pansy replied.

No, I belong with Jeb.

Remaining in one spot, weaving back and forth, was harder than it looked. She lost altitude and wobbled. The trees got closer, and she flapped frantically to rise, only it didn't quite work the way she wanted, and she kept sinking.

When the first branches struck, she tucked her wings, lest they tangle, and flailed her hands, looking for something to grip to stop her descent.

She banged off a few limbs before she managed to grab hold of one. There she dangled as an amused voice below said, "You can let go now."

"I don't want to fall!" she squeaked, eyes squeezed shut tight.

"You'll be fine. And you can take that to the Jones bank."

Trusting in him, like she'd trust in Jeb, she let go and dropped maybe two feet before hitting the ground. She opened a cautious eye, then both, to see she was unharmed, on solid land, and surrounded by a bunch of big, burly men.

Another brother with Jeb's wide grin faced her. "Well, hot damn. Jeb never told us he had a girlfriend who could fly."

She could have told them it was only her second time, but she was more worried about Jeb. "Where is he?"

"Kole's taken him prisoner. We aim to get him back."

"How can I help?"

When they told her the conditions, trade herself for Jeb, she agreed without hesitation. "I'll do it."

And she didn't change her mind when they arrived on the agreed-upon tarmac, Jeb in handcuffs and ankle tethers, his face twisted and angry.

"How dare you fucking do this?" he yelled at his brothers. "I trusted you to keep her safe."

As she walked past him toward the woman in red, she reached out to touch him, conscious of the red spots, laser sights, on his skin.

She whispered, "I trust you."

Save me.

❧ 22 ❧

THE RAGE and anguish as she walked away had Jeb bellowing. It didn't help he was stuck in his stupid human form, his mum having administered something to him that caused him to be unable to shift. The manacles between his ankles prevented him from doing more than a shuffle.

Despite the many rifle sights trained on him, he wanted to do something.

Act now before it's too late.

She said she trusted him. Then why did she go like a bird to the slaughter?

His brothers surrounded him, gripping him by the arms, murmuring, "Sorry, we had no choice."

No choice? Why couldn't they grasp he was willing to give his life for her?

The anger burned hotly inside him that they'd done this to Nev. He glowered as they ushered him inside their private jet.

Glared as they prepped for takeoff. The moment the cuffs on his wrists came off he swung.

Jackson caught his fist. "Calm down, little bro. We'll explain everything once we get out of here."

Explain what? He'd lost Nev.

Jeb stared out the window as the plane holding his angel departed the strip, heading off who knew where.

The seat beside him creaked as his brother Jeremy dropped into it. "You look like something the dingo dragged in."

"Since when do we negotiate with terrorists?" Jeb snarled.

"Didn't negotiate. Mum wanted the girl. The girl agreed."

"You should have said no," Jeb yelled. "You didn't need to hand her over to retrieve me." Especially considering he had a tracker inside his body they could have used to find him.

"You're right. We didn't. We knew where you were. Some abandoned warehouse with a basement."

Jeb blinked. "And you didn't save me because?"

"Da said we needed the coordinates for Mum's headquarters. And your girlfriend was kind enough to agree to help us out."

"Excuse me?" Because Jeb suddenly didn't understand anything at all.

"Simple. We knew Mum had another location. When you disappeared a week ago—"

"A week!" Why did it not seem like more than a few hours, a day at most?

What happened to me while I was unconscious?

"Yes, a week. At first, we couldn't find you. We thought you were dead. You should have seen Da going on a lunatic rampage."

Nice to know his dad cared.

"Then, about a day ago, your signal suddenly appeared in that abandoned warehouse. We immediately went scouting, only to realize it was just a decoy location. At the same time, we got the ransom demand."

"And thought it was a good plan to hand Nev over."

"She volunteered. Girl has got the hots for you something fierce."

Did she love him? It explained the words she'd whispered as she walked past him, head held high.

"She'll make you a great mate."

Anger had Jeb shaking his head. "How do you figure that? Mum took her, and I doubt she's just gonna hand her back."

"Which is why your girl is wearing a tracker. One in her clothes. And one in her body. Jaycon"—Jeremy pointed a finger toward the cockpit—"is watching to see where they end up."

"Mum's not stupid." Obviously, given how long she'd evaded their detection. "She'll be looking for one."

"Yup. And, when she finds the one in Nev's clothes, will toss it."

"What if she does something to the one in her body?"

"Then we might have a dilemma."

Except things played out as they'd hoped. The clothes were tossed from the helicopter, but the main chip in Nev herself kept beeping. They followed it.

Followed it all the way to Thailand, where they had to coast low to avoid radar and ghost their way into the country.

Their connections around the world meant they had a place to land and stash the jet, along with a set of wheels to continue their pursuit.

They spent only a few hours getting ready. Long hours that Jeb itched about.

Each minute Nev was in his mum's custody was a minute they could be hurting her.

This rescue was taking too long, and yet, at the same time, he understood they couldn't go in halfcocked. Rescuing Nev in one piece was the most important thing.

As dusk fell, they put their plan in motion. His entire family had come. They were spread out around the concrete bunker-like building housing his angel. Or at least the signal they hoped she still wore.

The place certainly seemed correct given the guards on the roof and the searchlights constantly moving around the building. The red eyes of cameras watching.

It wouldn't be enough. Jeb was here to save Nev, and no fancy defense system would stand in his way. While Nev was his main focus, he understood his brothers, the uncles, and his da had another target in mind.

First, though, they had to get into the building.

"My turn." Shove. A body jostled to take his position.

"No, it's my turn." Push. Another brother tried to take his place.

"Screw you both, I'm next." Time to assert himself before he got shuffled to the back.

Whack. "Shut up, you morons. Before you let them know we're here." Uncle Kendrick glared at his nephews, Jebediah, Jeremy, and Jakob. Given he'd whooped their butts more than once when they'd gotten out of line—*Who smoked my last cigar??*—the brothers stopped jostling to take point. Despite the danger, they were all eager to go first. But none more than Jeb. The longer Angel was inside, the longer his mum had to do whatever evil shit she had planned.

Uncle Kendrick whipped out orders. "Jeb, take care of the guards at the door. Use the flash bang. You two idiots"—a finger jabbed at Jeb's brothers—"cover him. I don't want those snipers on the roof getting a shot off."

No one dared argue after that. The earplugs went in, and the safety goggles went on. Only morons dashed into a firefight without some kind of protection. Ringing ears weren't just unpleasant; they allowed the enemy to sneak up on a fellow.

Jeb still remembered the time Jaxon got too big for his britches and fired the shotgun several times in a row at a target then carried on like an idiot, whooping and hollering. Given it was three in the morning, not everyone was happy with his shenanigans. Uncle Kyle stomped up to the oblivious idiot and put a gun to Jeb's brother's head. Jax never forgot his earplugs again. He also never celebrated being a moron at 3:00 a.m. after that. Jaxon began looking into a non-military career and ended up some glorified forest ranger who protected animals. The family wasn't too surprised. Stupid bloke became a vegetarian after their first safari.

"Cover me, boys," Jeb said with a grin as he palmed the flash bang and waited for his cue behind the rusty yellow car they'd parked themselves behind just before dawn.

Given there wasn't much ground cover between the car and the building where the guards stood, armed with rifles, Jeb had to rely on blind luck—and a diversion. Across the way, something barked and howled. Then giggled. His other brothers, just as excited as Jeb about this mission.

The guys on the roof moved away from the edge.

While the ones at the door headed toward the noise.

His cue. Jeb ran out into the open, pulling the pin as he ran, drawing his arm back.

He launched the small missile. The stun grenade rolled in front of the blokes standing guard.

Not being all that bright, one of them leaned down for a closer peek. The other one had the brains to at least duck and cover his face.

Bang!

The grenade exploded in a bright flash, and the guard stumbled back, blinking and cursing. Just the opening they needed.

Jeb sprinted the last few yards for the door, his brothers only a few paces behind him. So much for giving him cover. But then again, Uncle Kendrick wouldn't let him down. None of his family would in this multi-prong attack. Judging by the distant bangs and shouts, his other family members infiltrated the far side of the bunker.

Shit was about to hit the fan.

Jeb reached the front of the building and its first line of defense. His fist flew, hitting the dazed guard right in the kisser before he could think to use his gun. Then again, in close proximity, guns weren't the right kind of weapon. Bruising fisticuffs though? He and his bros were pros.

The fellow dropped, and his partner soon followed, leaving the door free of obstacle. Seemed too easy, except Jeb knew better. A place doing illegal shit would, of course, be protected and locked up tighter than Fort Knox.

This might be a good time to admit he and his brothers had managed to make it into the heart of that old bullion depository and took a selfie in the vault, all because of a drunken dare. A Jones brothers adventure, which one day Jebediah might write about.

The stunned guards too quickly began lifting their heads when his brothers reached them.

Wham. A left hook caught one in the jaw, and the guard flew back, hitting the door of the building before he slumped. The other fellow took a few hits from his brother before joining him. Two down. A shit-ton more to go.

With Jakob watching the area around them, Jeb and Jeremy quickly knelt and pulled plastic ties from their cargo pants pockets to tether the hands of their first two prisoners. If things went to hell, the Joneses might need to question them later.

While they took care of the guards, Uncle Kendrick smushed a gray piece of clay onto the door where the handle met the frame.

This wasn't a place you could just walk in. Much like the Bunyip Institute, entry required retinal scans from living tissue. A pain in the arse if you had to enter or leave in a hurry. Much better to—

"Duck!" yelled his uncle.

"Goose!" teased Jeb as they all hit the ground.

Boom. The rumble vibrated the earth they lay on, the charge having blown open the door, giving them entry.

They didn't have time for subtle.

"Cover me," Jeb demanded, jumping to his feet, determined to be the first through the door. He pulled his gun, a snub-nosed piece not available for regular purchase in Australia—but he had connections—and eased the muzzle in first, a tease for anyone watching. Only idiots charged in.

Jakob, the family idiot, kicked at the remains of the door and ran in yelling.

He didn't drop dead of a gunshot, probably on account he still was coasting off the luck of that rabbit's foot he'd shoved up his arse as a kid. Done on a dare, and yet, the bastard seemed to have more than his fair share of good chance.

Since Jakob cleared the way, they entered behind him, guns raised, ready to shoot anything that moved. Taking prisoners was all well and good as long as they weren't in danger.

"Clear," Jeremy noted. The door they'd blown open led to a tight vestibule area, ten by ten, with nothing but a desk and...

Movement caught Jeb's eye, and he aimed his gun at the fellow standing up from behind the reception area.

Jeb's 'roo instincts took over and he bounced, flying over the desk to land on the guard. He punched him a few times in the face and heard bone crunch.

While the man wailed—humans ever were whiny when they got a booboo—Jeb kept moving knowing Jeremy would handle the guard with more of the plastic ties. Jakob had his back. As for their uncle...

Kendrick tapped at his wrist communication unit and said absently, "You boys go ahead. I'm gonna make sure no one gets past me here."

They exited the vestibule and were confronted by several doors. Where did they go? Behind which one was Angel? Jaycon hadn't had time before the mission to pull up any building schematics. They were going in blind.

Common sense dictated they stick together for more firepower. But they had to work fast. By now, their mum would know they'd come for Nev—and revenge. Who knew what that woman would do?

A distant rumble let him know more of his family breached the rear.

"We have to get moving," stated Jeremy, joining them. "I'll take the door in front of us"

Whereas Jeb went left and Jakob right. Behind the door, Jeb discovered a short hallway that went for several paces before ending in another portal. No surprise, it also had a lock.

Should have dragged the guard with me. It required an eyeball for entry. Or a bomb.

The chunk of explosive he placed blew the lock enough that he could yank it open, but he didn't immediately rush through. By now the guards in this place would be warned. And holes in his body? Not conducive to good health.

He pulled another stun grenade from his pocket, one-handed because of his gun. He used his teeth to pull the pin.

He eased open the door, just enough for him to roll the grenade in. Crouching low saved him from the gunfire that erupted.

"Is that all you got?" he yelled as the door swung shut. He turned from the blast, closing his eyes behind his safety goggles. The earplugs didn't completely muffle the sound of the explosion.

His eyewear, however, protected him from the acrid smoke he'd unleashed. He crab-walked into the next room, his inner 'roo not at all happy about the smoke in a confined place. But not all fights could be out in the open.

Given he couldn't see two feet in front of him, he tucked away his gun in favor of his fists. Didn't want an accident. Uncle Kyle still glared at Kevyn each time they got together. The scar on his ass had left a permanent dimple.

Ping. Someone fired from within the smoky fog.

Jeb fired back blindly and was rewarded with a yelp. He kept sidling along the wall. As he came across doors, he secured them rather than going inside. Part of their mission was to keep as much of the building, and its research, as intact as possible. The shifter high council would want details on what occurred here to ensure it wasn't repeated and, according to Uncle Kevyn, so they could help the victims recover.

That was the plausible excuse given, and yet, Jeb had to wonder. Shouldn't anything Frankenstein-ish be destroyed lest someone be tempted to take up where previous attempts left off? After all, by all indications Kole —and his mum—were inspired by a certain American mastermind who'd had visions of grandeur. Literally. Turned out the original mad scientist was some kind of rodent that wanted to become a predator. That didn't end well...for her.

Some people just weren't happy with the lot they got in life. Jeb was perfectly fine being a kangaroo. It came with agility, strength, and good looks. He didn't need anything more. Except for his angel.

Pop.

Someone hadn't given up. Jeb fired off a shot. It wasn't answered. He kept creeping along the hall, and at each door he found, he wedged an expander in the seam. A cool thing Jaycon had found when attending the last Spy Tech convention. An object resembling a small marble, all he had to do was press it against the seam of a door and the floor, then spit on it. Any kind of moisture made it expand, filling in the crack and then instantly hardening, sealing off entrances. Someone could still blow through it, but given that would make noise, he'd have warning if someone tried to sneak up behind him.

The hallway finally ended just as the smoke began to dissipate. He found the lone guard slumped on the floor in a bloody puddle. Oops. This one wouldn't be talking.

Since the hallway appeared clear, he stood and noted the door he'd found at the end of the hall had a sign indicating stairs.

He tapped his earpiece, activating the microphone, and muttered, "West hallway, first floor clear."

It took a moment before his earpiece crackled. "Hold position. Wait for backup."

Wait. Easy for Jaycon to say. He was in the command van just outside the hidden lab's perimeter.

Jeb's blood was running hot. Too hot to sit still, especially since he could hear gunfire coming from the floors above him.

Were they shooting their prisoners? He couldn't take that chance.

"I think I hear something. Heading to the stairs."

He then tapped his earpiece to mute it and smirked as Jaycon hollered, "Moron. Wait for help. The second floor is on a separate system, and I haven't hacked into it yet."

And? It wasn't like they were sneaking in at this point. Waiting could cost them.

Unlike the other doors, the stairwell wasn't locked and gave easily. A firm shove sent it slamming against the wall, and he aimed his gun.

Nothing to see.

Bummer.

He crept up the stairs, gun pointed, and could have shouted with glee when he heard the scuff of boots overhead. Finally, some action.

He crept up, keeping quiet so as to not give warning, but he needn't have bothered. He saw the boot first, dangling from the edge of the landing for the second floor. The body it belonged to lay prone, occasionally jiggling as the last of the blood and life eked from it. Something had done a number on the guard.

A peek through the busted door showed more bodies. Bleeding. Broken. Dead.

What happened here?

It was then he caught it, amidst the scent of violence, a hint of something beautiful. Pure. And somehow twisted.

Angel?

She'd been through here. Obviously not a victim of the violence, not yet. Had one of their experiments gotten loose?

Just in case he was wrong about her scent, he went through the door to take a closer look at the bodies and what they'd guarded. The second floor reminded him a lot of the last institute he'd raided. It held about a half-dozen cells—three oversized cages on each side, the welded metal rods only wide enough to shove a hand through.

Inside the cages…

"Ah, shit," he cursed. Seemed he'd just found some of the test subjects. About five of them at any rate. The one in the cage closest to him more octopus than man, the too human eyes—a bright blue—bobbing in a gelatinous mass that shook with rage.

The thing—because sympathy couldn't go as far as calling it him—oozed toward the bars, jelly arms flailing, but stopped short of touching them. Good thing, because if it came after Jeb, he wasn't too sure how to kill it. He'd left the flamethrower in the truck.

A few more steps and he got to see the next test subject. Some kind of lizard-man, it's body a mishmash of reptile parts. It hissed. He hissed back.

The other cages held other impossible creatures. None of them able to speak in words. None of them human.

And then he saw the final cage, the one with the bars twisted and bent enough that someone could escape. Feathers were scattered on the floor.

The scent?

"Angel." He whispered her name. What had happened?

It was then he heard it. A screeching scream of rage that somehow echoed throughout the building and goosed his skin.

He went running for the door and the stairs, intent on going up. Because when the cry faded, he caught the sound of a helicopter preparing for takeoff.

BOVIARY WAS RIGHT when he said people had a unique scent, and now that Nev knew to look for it, it wasn't hard to follow.

The cell was a bit tricky to escape, the bars sizzling her skin. But her anger wasn't about to let them stand in her away. Especially since she still felt the sting of the needles entering her skin.

Not even a prisoner a few minutes on the plane and they were filling her full of poison.

They'd put her to sleep, and she awoke in a cell.

In a foul mood.

A mood that exploded when she inhaled the perfume of that woman.

Her.

The one who wanted to hurt Jeb.

Once the bars bent, the red haze helped her through the obstacles in her path. They stood in the way of the smell she tracked.

It went all the way to the rooftop. Emerging on the top

of the building, Nev didn't even look as a body lunged at her.

Crack.

Necks were fragile things.

She cocked her head as she observed the slender column of her target. It wouldn't take much pressure to break.

"You." Nev pointed a finger with a rather longish nail at the end. Black, too, despite the fact she'd not had them painted in ages.

The lady in red never lost her cool, but she did bark an order to the men flanking her. "Shoot the subject."

The darts hit, spreading their drug, and Nev sank to her knees. Damn it. Not now. She was so close to her revenge. So close to making the world a safer place.

She put out her hands so she wouldn't splat on her face. She couldn't focus on anything but the bright red pumps Jeb's mama wore.

"Well, you were more trouble than it was worth. You led the boys to me."

Despite the sluggishness in her veins, Nev managed a crooked smile. "I did. Tracker."

"Smart. But easy enough to take care of when we're in the air. Get in the chopper."

"N-no." She managed to stutter the word as she lifted her head.

"Get in the chopper or you and those curs who carry my blood will die." The lady in red held up a small device with an antenna. "One push of this button and you'll all go kaboom."

"Your kids."

"Those boys have been a never-ending source of annoyance. So don't think I won't push it."

The threat moved Nev's leaden legs. She staggered closer, aware of the guards with their weapons trained on her. Waiting to pump her full of more narcotics.

She wobbled and blinked, her eyes losing focus.

"Hold out your hands," the woman ordered. "Tie her."

A swaying Nev didn't resist as the plastic strands went around her wrists and were cinched.

"Load her in the chopper. Time to go."

Hands grabbed at Nev and thrust her inside, not taking care to be gentle. But she welcomed the pain. It helped ease some of the numbness from the drugs.

Jeb's evil mama tossed the device to her henchman. "Once we've cleared the building, blow it up."

But... "Jeb." The word croaked from Nev, and a single tear managed to drop.

"Is in the building and will probably die. Or not. You never know with those damned Joneses. They're a stubborn lot. In a way, I kind of hope Jeb makes it out. I'm sure he would jump at a chance to be reunited with you. To help me take the next step in our experiments."

"He won't help you." The words were pushed past a thick tongue.

"Maybe he won't want to, not at first, but there are ways of making him bend."

The implication was clear. And horrifying.

"You can't hurt him."

"I won't do it myself. But he will bow to my will and do as he's told or suffer."

The fact that this mother could so coldly speak of hurting her son, her child, roused the memories of Nev's own youth. How her daddy liked to hurt her.

"No," she said, the word but a soft whisper. "No." It

emerged louder and stronger, if unheard over the now roaring engine of the helicopter blades.

The rage grew stronger each time she said it. "No." It burned in her veins. "No." She wouldn't allow it to happen. Hadn't there been enough pain already?

It's time someone else felt the pain, the dark voice inside spoke, the words wrapping around her consciousness, soothing her with a promise. *I can make this right.*

Let me in. Let me take care of you.

Give in to her darkness? Yet what other choice did she have?

Fix this. Save us. Save Jeb.

The darkness flowed over her with cool calm and determination.

Strength pulsed inside her, burning away the drugs. Her muscles tensed, and the tether at her wrists broke with a firm tug. She stood inside the large helicopter.

Free.

Angry.

And finally, no longer a half-breed.

Her voice was terrible when she screamed.

THE CHOPPER HAD BARELY RISEN from the roof when Jeb heard the shriek. It raised the hair on his body, pimpled his flesh, and made his blood run cold.

"Angel." He murmured her name and stared up at the sky. Too late.

Or was he?

The machine in the air wobbled, as if something happened on board. The windshield blew outward, and a body came flying out. The pilot. Immediately, the chopper began to list.

"Oh shit." Jeb ran for the edge of the rooftop knowing there was nothing he could do, and yet he couldn't help but follow.

"Jump," he shouted. "Dammit, Angel. Get out of there!" Before it crashed. They could fix broken bones, but they couldn't—

Boom! The chopper hit the ground, the impact enough to make everything around them shudder. The blades screeched and whined as they kept trying to turn. Smoke began to billow, and he could only watch, helpless, as it

176

exploded, sending chunks of metal flying. He shielded his face only for a moment before looking again.

Looking for any signs of a survivor.

He dropped to his knees as the billowing smoke and flames filled the air.

His brother, he didn't know or care which one, clapped a hand on his shoulder. "Sorry."

Such an inadequate word to describe his anguish.

"Kreeeeee!" The scream wasn't his, even if it bubbled inside. His head lifted and lifted some more until he stared overhead at the dark angel descending from the heavens.

His angel. Who looked terrifying.

But alive.

Her eyes blazed, her skin was drawn and gray, her lip curled back over fangs, and her fingers, long, curved talons, but he'd never seen anything more beautiful.

"Angel." He held out his arms even as his brother whistled, "Are ye feckin' nuts?"

Yes. He was. Nuts for this woman.

For a moment, he wondered if she'd hug or eviscerate him.

Then there was no wondering for she threw herself at him, her arms wrapping around him, sobs wracking her body while he held her, whispering soothing words. "It's okay. You're safe." Which was all that mattered.

"She was gonna kill you," Nev murmured against his skin.

"Now she can't hurt anyone." Because no way had anyone survived the inferno.

While his brothers handled the cleanup of the building, Jeb took Angel away. Took her to a safe place owned by a friend, the blanket over her head and shoulders doing much to hide her wings.

The first thing he did was put her in a shower.

The hot streaming water helped ease her out of the shock she was in.

"Jeb," she said, murmuring his name against his skin.

"I'm here, Angel."

"The plan worked."

"It did, and I'm going on the record as saying right now, if you ever do something—"

"I would do it again if it meant saving you." She pulled away from him.

"I'm not worth that kind of sacrifice, Angel."

"You are to me." She ducked her head.

He tilted her chin. "Aren't we a fine pair? Both wanting to one-up the other when it comes to being the most in love."

Her jaw dropped. "I never said…"

"But I am going to say it. I love you, Nevaeh, and I'm sorry. I should have told you everything in the treehouse, but I was—"

"—a man."

The corners of his eyes crinkled as he smiled. "I was. And I'll probably do more stupid things in the future, but despite that, I hope you'll stay with me."

"But what about these?" She ruffled her wings, sending droplets of water smattering against the curtain and wall.

"If we have to live in a remote mountain range for you to be able to go about freely, then so be it. I love you, Angel. Say you'll be my mate."

He assumed by the kiss it was a yes.

Her lips hungrily devoured his as their hot breaths mingled. Slippery tongues danced, and her body molded to his.

He let his hands roam her body, stripping her sodden

clothes, skimming down her flanks then up, over bare skin.

On her back.

He blinked then blinked again in case there was water in his eyes.

But there was nothing wrong with his sight.

"Um, Angel. Your wings are gone."

"What?" She whirled around as if she could see and, when she couldn't, jumped out of the shower sopping wet.

She crowed as she peeked in the mirror. "They're gone!"

For now. He'd wager they'd come back, but for the moment... He swept her into his arms and carried her to the bed.

He tossed her on it, and she squealed as she bounced.

"Jeb!"

"Right here, Angel."

He covered her body with his own, his mouth finding hers, their passion a torrent of heat and need.

Jeb couldn't content himself with only her lips. He went exploring the column of her throat, licking and nipping the flesh. Teasing her with soft caresses. He bit the flesh pulsing in time to her heartbeat.

Her breathing hitched, and hands stroked at his shoulders. Her bare breasts rubbed against his chest, her nipples taut, protruding buds that begged for his touch.

He kissed his way down to them, lavishing those tips with attention. Drawing them into his mouth and sucking. Letting them go that he might swirl his tongue around them.

Only when she writhed and moaned with her eyes closed did he move lower, rubbing his face on the soft skin of her belly.

He thrust an arm under her buttocks, hoisting her high enough to expose her pink and moist sex to his view.

He fanned his hot breath over her tender skin and watched her tremble. The wet tip of his tongue traced the outer edges of her nether lips. Teasing her. Arousing...

He licked her, a long, wet swipe of his tongue against her sensitive flesh. She writhed against his mouth as he lapped at her. When his lips latched onto her clit, she bucked and cried.

"Please," she begged.

"Anything my angel desires," were the rumbly words murmured against her sex.

He moved over her until the head of his cock brushed against her. He probed the entrance to her sex, wanting to prolong the moment.

But she was impatient. She grabbed him around the hips and surged upward, sheathing his shaft.

He dug his fingers into her hips as she squeezed him. Angled his hips to go deeper.

He thrust his way in and out of her, each slap of flesh drawing a moan from his angel. As he increased his pace, her breathing came faster and faster. Her fingers dug at the sheets.

Their bodies moved in rhythm. And even though it was considered kind of old school, and very outback, at the moment of climax, he bit her. Wouldn't you know, she bit him harder.

EPILOGUE

WEEKS LATER...

It had been weeks since the crash. Weeks of being with the man Nev loved. A man who'd helped her get a second chance at life.

Real life. Not the kind hidden or in a cage because she was now in control of her body.

Slowly but surely, she was getting the hang of not only flying but also hiding her wings. They'd spent some time with Maisy, who had been a big help, not allowing Nev to give up. The two of them often getting into yelling spats, but in the end, it worked. Nev could pass as human again, which, for some reason, seemed to cause Jeb some worry.

"What's wrong?" she asked, draping herself on his lap. They currently lived at the ranch, which she struggled with at first, not used to having so many people around, but she had to admit it was growing on her. Having several big brothers looking out for her did a lot for her sense of security. And their spats provided entertainment.

"Guess you don't need to run away with me anymore."

"Nope."

"You can be anywhere you want."

"Yup."

She did it on purpose to tease him until finally she laughed. She cupped his cheeks. "Silly man. You're not seriously worried I'm going to leave, are you? I love you." Loved him in spite of the fact that his mother had changed her. In spite of his brothers and the other males in his family who seemed to think loud and rough was how to show affection.

At least with each other. With Nev and the other ladies, they were very well behaved.

But that didn't stop Nev from spending time on the internet, poring over images of treehouses. Lavish ones.

Forcing Jeb to ask, "What are you doing?"

"Research for our new home."

"Ours?"

"Yes, ours." And with that word, he finally relaxed.

"Guess it's true what they say. Set someone free and they give you the best blowjobs ever."

"Is that a hint?" she asked with a smile.

"Was hoping for a reality."

Except they didn't have time to get busy. His phone buzzed, the screen showing a one-line text message.

Turn on the news.

Frowning, he reached for the remote and flipped the channel. Both their jaws might have slammed to the floor as they recognized the woman on screen.

"Um, is that your mother?" she asked.

"Yeah."

The woman they thought dead? Again. "Who is that with her?" asked Nev, pointing her finger.

"…exciting developments at the Bunyip Institute. Meet the future of science," said Jeb's mum to the reporters gathered. "Perfect children." A pair of whom stared at the camera with the same vivid blue eyes and smiled at the same time. "With upgrades."

"What do you mean by upgrades?" asked a reporter.

And that was when the twins—a pair of girls, their hair long, red and straight—suddenly had wings burst from their backs before they took flight.

"Oh shit."

※

MAISY FLIPPED OFF THE TELLY, STILL FROWNING AT THE NEWS.

The ex-Mrs. Jones had done it, divulged secrets endangering them all. The world wasn't ready for the cryptids to emerge. Not ready for monsters.

What would this announcement mean?

A brisk knock at her door raised her head. Only one reason for anyone to be coming to her this late at night. Someone needed her help.

Wrapping her sweater more tightly around her body, she ignored the bristling of her inner feline to grab the shotgun that never left her side.

Saving lives was one thing. Protecting herself, another.

Pausing behind her door, a thick wooden affair that could withstand even the rampaging kick of a kanga, she hit the intercom button and said, "Who is it?"

The reply, just one word, sent a chill through her.

"Jakob."

She opened her mouth to tell him to leave. She wasn't ready to deal with him yet. She might never be ready.

But then he said the magic words she couldn't ignore. "I need help."

THE END?
MAYBE. MAYBE NOT.

Visit EveLanglais.com for more books.
Check out a new series coming summer of 2019.

57579739R00111

Made in the USA
Middletown, DE
31 July 2019